Mars, Ho!

From the author of *Nobots*

Cover photos: NASA/JPL
ISBN 978-0-9910531-5-5
Printed in the United States of America

Acknowledgments

To Dewey Green, who suggested that I write a book about whores in space and asked that a character be named after him, and Felber's Tavern, where the idea originated and where parts of it were written.

To slashdot.org and soylentnews.org, where I posted the rough first draft, and to their communities who offered helpful comments to the draft.

To Mark Twain, who introduced us to a first person telling by an uneducated person.

To Google for help with translations.

Table of Contents

Chapter One

Meeting

"Come in, Charles. Did you bring Knolls' report?"

"Sure did, Dewey, here it is," the company president said, taking a small chip out of his pocket and handing it to the CEO.

These two were the highest ranking members of the solar system's largest shipping and transportation company. Together they had built the company from scratch, and between the two of them they held enough stock to completely control the company. It not only shipped people and goods, but also was the largest shipbuilding company as well. They built the ships and other machinery needed, and sold or leased the machinery, houseboats, and other small boats to private and government entities. They had been approached by various governments to construct warships, but had declined the offers. War is bad for the shipping business, it makes everything dangerous and expensive.

"Did you read it?" the CEO asked.

"Yes, I did, It took me all day yesterday, but there's a much shorter version on your chip as well as the version I read. I'd skip the long version.

"It's interesting, Knolls could be a writer if his grammar wasn't so atrocious. It was actually a good read otherwise, these reports are usually pretty dry. I hate reading most of them, but I didn't mind this one at all."

"Well, Knolls is just a ship's captain. It's not like he's been to college or anything. How detailed is the report?"

"Heh, too detailed in places, I had them delete the days

that didn't really give us any information. I didn't really need to hear about his bowel movements, but most are still in the short version. Like I said, there are two copies, but the shorter one is the one I'd read if I were you."

"How much did Knolls leave out?"

"Nothing important. At least I don't think he left anything important out. All the important stuff is in the short version, anyway. But I'll tell you, Dewey, this company has some serious problems we weren't aware of. This report was invaluable. We have a lot of work ahead of us."

"I heard he saved her life? Is that correct?"

"Yes, it is indeed, her life and everyone else's lives. He apparently kept a cool head, kept his wits about him and did everything right, even if he didn't always go exactly by the book. The times he didn't go by the book should be in the book, though. They were downright strokes of genius sometimes, plain common sense other times. Knolls is pretty sharp. It looks like he saved Kelly's ship and cargo as well as his own more than once by using his head and not going by the book. I'm pretty sure that when you've read it you'll agree that we need to change some policies and regulations."

"Yes, I read the draft of the preliminary investigation report. Sabotage to Kelly's ship during the Mars overhaul so they could get his ship and ores. One of the workers was arrested, he'd been paid a huge sum of cash to do it. It wasn't very hard to catch him, they just looked at spending patterns to find who was living beyond their means. He confessed, but we need to figure out how to prevent that from happening again. They won't have the final report until Kelly gets back to Mars and they can examine the ship's systems."

"We're on it already, old buddy. If Mark Johnson can't solve it, it's insoluble."

"It had better not be."

"I sure can't argue with that. If we can't find a solution we're in serious trouble."

"What were damages to cargo?"

2

"Well, one specimen was severely injured in a fire but recovered long before reaching the port on Mars. A few of the specimens got into physical altercations but there was no lasting damage to them. The worst were some pretty bad accidental self-inflicted cuts from an encounter with pirates, but the damage was far less than we expected; we were pretty sure there would be quite a few fatalities, considering how dangerous the cargo was that was being shipped.

"A passenger associated with the company that hired us had a severe concussion, several broken ribs, and a dislocated shoulder as a result of interacting with their dangerous cargo, but was out of sick bay before the ship docked at the repair facility. She's still recovering. She should get some kind of a medal, read the report. We underestimated just how dangerous that cargo was. It was actually a good thing Knolls had that cargo or he'd be dead and pirates would have our ship."

"Yes, we have to find a way to stop the piracy, there's way too much loss of life and loss of our property. I'm going to look into that myself."

"I agree, and we should have started Ramos' fleet a lot sooner, that's a good start. It's hard to get that stubborn Griffins to understand the need for security; he doesn't like spending the money. I ordered a report from Ramos and am thinking about ordering that all captains write a report after every run, although not as detailed as Knolls'."

"Were there any other damages?" the CEO asked.

"One of the ship's two fusion reactors was ruined and will have to be rebuilt, as well as three of its ion drives. More most likely would have blown, and maybe all of them, if Knolls hadn't shut the two down that were next to the three ruined ones. That's not in the book, either, but Engineering tells me it should be. Two repairbots were destroyed while attempting to repair the first thruster that shorted out.

"The other fusion generator was damaged but easily repaired once he got a replacement regulator from Ramos. One battery was incinerated and one docking ring was badly damaged. Minimal damage considering the dangerous cargo it was carrying and the problems Knolls encountered. That battery was a great idea, even though it did damage the docking ring. I don't think any of our captains ever faced anywhere near as many pirates on one trip, let alone that huge swarm that almost got him. There sure was a nasty mess in the ship's engine section. May I ask, Dewey, why you allowed her on board with such a dangerous cargo?"

"Allow her? She's going to do whatever the hell she wants no matter what I think. She seldom even writes. I'm just glad it turned out as well as it did."

"Sorry, that isn't any of my business. Anyway, I hope you read that report. It answers a lot of questions the investigators didn't."

"Don't worry, I will, you can be sure of it. Afternoon open? Want to shoot nine holes?"

"Of course. But please, Dewey, read the report first."

"Don't worry, I've been looking forward to it, especially considering... get the hell out of here, Charles. Let me read this thing and I'll see you on the golf course. I can't spend the whole afternoon there, though, just nine holes and lunch. My afternoon is pretty full."

"Okay, I'll meet you in the clubhouse about... ten or ten thirty maybe?"

"Sounds good to me. See you there, Charles." He put the chip in his tablet and started reading.

Chapter Two

Report

I don't know why in the hell they're making me write this damned report, I ain't never had to write no dumb report before. Ain't like I ever been to college or nothing. I didn't even have to write no report after Vesta, why now? People died on that trip, nobody but pirates died on this one. Maybe it was the pirates, I never saw so many God damned pirates, nowhere near that giant swarm of them. Maybe because of the droppers. Maybe because this trip was so damned out of the ordinary in so many other ways? I don't know, I'm just talking into this thing and I don't know where to start, so I'll just start.

I was scared shitless – the CEO had called me into his office. Jesus, the fucking CEO! Why would a CEO want a lowly boat captain to talk to him? Yeah, decades ago ship's captains were really important guys, but that was back when they needed crews, and captains needed to be smart and educated. I was just a glorified bus driver and babysitter. My old buddy Bill is still a space trucker, he likes being alone, he's kind of a nerd. Me, I hate it. Especially after Titan.

I liked hauling passengers because at least I'd have somebody to talk to. It takes a long time to get from planet to planet, especially from Earth to the gas giants because you usually don't have any passengers or live animals so your gravity is less, making it take longer, and it's usually a boring trip. They pay pretty damned good, too – cargo boats don't need babysitters. Plus you usually don't have much gravity on a cargo ship unless the company that hires us to haul their cargo pays an extra, expensive fee, so you need to spend more time in a centrifuge when you get back to Earth after not having much gravity for such a long time. They really have to be in a hurry for that. Boats carrying passengers or animals had pretty comfortable gravity, though. I hear that's one reason our company is number one, because our boats are faster and have higher gravity than the other companies' ships. But carrying passengers is a lot shorter trip to anywhere because of the gravity.

Jesus! The CEO! I was shaking as I walked into his office, I was so scared. If I was going to get fired for that little incident on Vesta my chief would have sacked me. I didn't know what to think.

"Have a seat, Mister Knolls. Coffee?" he said.

"Uh," I replied, "Uh, yes sir, thank you, sir." I fidgeted in my chair. His assistant gave me a cup and I took a sip; it was really good coffee, better than I could make. Too bad the robots can't make coffee like that, robot coffee is really nasty.

"Knolls, your supervisor's manager told me all about Vesta."

I was quaking in my boots and almost pissed my pants. Shit, they were going to prosecute me for killing those two idiots.

"That was some damned good work, Mister Knolls."

My head kind of exploded. "Sir? Two men died!"

"Yes, Mister Knolls, but you saved two hundred million dollars in equipment and another forty five million in cargo, plus our shipping charges, and the wrongful death suits only cost a million each. We could have beaten them in court; it was their own damned fault, after all. Those two were really stupid, but fighting it would have cost the company more, according to our legal staff. God damned good work, Mister Knolls!"

"Uh, thank you, sir," I said, wondering how damned evil this man could be. I'd just been trying to save my own ass, there wasn't any saving those two morons, they would have died no matter what I did. I still felt bad about it, though.

"I have a new assignment for you," he said. "Your

supervisor's manager told me you didn't like cargo runs and why, but this time you'll have someone to talk to."

My head kind of stopped working right then, if it was even working before. He said "This assignment is important. You're the perfect man for this job and we're giving you a fifty percent raise to do it, and Vesta was part of the calculations. You're a very good captain, Mister Knolls. One of our best."

"Uh, thank you, sir. Uh, what's my cargo supposed to be and where am I taking it?" I asked.

The CEO smiled. "Women. You're to transport two hundred woman to Mars."

"Women?" I asked, my brain still not working right. Women as cargo? I didn't get it.

"Prostitutes, Mister Knolls."

Taking a couple hundred whores to Mars? Wow!

"So, Mister Knolls, are you taking the assignment?"

What could I say except yes? Of course, not ever having met any whores I had no idea how much of a pain in the ass it would be or that I would regret my decision, which I actually started regretting before we even left the ground, when I met Tammy. I wish they would have warned me how dangerous this trip and my cargo was going to be, I'd have retired right then and there. Probably why they didn't. Of course, they didn't know how damned many pirates I'd have to fight off. I'm glad I did now or I probably wouldn't have met Destiny, but the trip itself sure sucked. Except when I was with her.

"Yes, sir, how could I not? Of course! When do I leave?" I said stupidly.

I wish my brain would have been working. God, what a mistake I made. I should have just retired right then and there, I have a little savings and I have my houseboat. Even if I'd have to start printing some stuff out instead of buying it, and I suck at printing stuff out.

Like I said, the trip was nothing but trouble. Well, almost... like I said, there was Destiny. But most of the trip was more horrible than I could imagine. Especially when we got closer to Mars and the monsters and pirates came out.

Chapter three

Tamatha

What got me interested, of course, was the fact that they were *whores!* I was going to be carrying a boatload of horny whores! It was like Christmas in June, what a Christmas present two hundred whores were going to be! What a party I was going to have! Ho, ho, ho!

See, I'm not good with women. Not good at all, not the least little bit. What I mean by that is women use me and I'm too damned stupid to see it. And I was too damned stupid to realize that whores are women.

What happened earlier, you know, led to my stupidity. Well, except the stupidity of not realizing whores are women, that was incredibly stupid.

Did I tell you about women? They've made my life hell. Look at the week on Earth before they handed me that Mars assignment, for instance. Hell, look what my ex-wife put me through. No, never mind, you don't want to hear it. Sorry. I'll try to stay on topic.

Anyway, being stupid, I was happy. I guess that's the secret to happiness – be stupid. But stupid pays later, I found out. Almost as bad as stupid is ignorant, but at least you can cure ignorant.

I went home, took a shower, and checked out Ol' Miss real good before I went out single party partying. I had to make sure the old gal was doing well, she's home, after all. They had just raised her to the top of the tube earlier in the day and I wanted to make sure they hadn't damaged her. After checking her out I decided to hit a bar.

I called a cab, and a large black Checker rolled up shortly. I told it to take me to the nearest bar, that my fone said was five miles away. Why in the hell are all the bars so far away from spaceports? I swear, I'm going to open a bar right outside a spaceport. I'll clean up!

I should have had it take me to the cheapest bar. Live and learn, I guess. Or maybe not, I forgot and went back to the same damned bar the next night. Like I said, you can't cure stupid.

I got to the bar. It had a big sign out front, "Suzie's Sports Bar". Not a bad bar, except it was almost empty, and I found out when I paid the bar tab it was expensive as hell. Two guys were shooting pool, three more guys in business suits going over some paper. Real paper like they make from hemp, not a tablet. Paper... how quaint. A couple at another table and two old women at the bar. And it was a big place, had a whole bunch of holographic video screens, five pool tables, ten dart boards, a bunch of video games and twenty kinds of beer on tap. Really nice bar, but damn but their beer cost a lot.

Beer. I reminded myself to stop on the way back to Ol' Miss and get a lot of beer, 'cause this was going to be a long trip. Oh, hell, I'll just order it on my fone and have it shipped to Ol' Miss, I can get a lot more that way. Better too much than not enough.

I pulled out the fone and ordered the beer, it'll be there waiting for me inside the gantry lift when I get home.

Uh, you guys *really* need to know about the bars I went to before I left? Well, okay, even though I can't understand why. I ordered a draft. Huh? You want that much detail? Okay, it was a Newcastle. What? I don't know, I ain't no beer snob. I can't tell a lager from a pilsner. Really? Lager comes in green bottles, pilsner in brown and ale in clear bottles? Well, that's interesting but it didn't come from a bottle, it was a draft and it came in a mug.

Whoever was playing the jukebox was playing that crap twelve year olds listen to, so I put a dime in, played some classical music from way back in the twentieth century and hit "yes" when it asked me if I wanted the song to play next. That cost a nickle, but *Rhapsody in Blue* was half a cent and it's a really long song. Stupid kids pay a nickle to hear that crappy new music that's under copyright and the songs are only two or three minutes long. I had it play *Rap City in Blues* from the first half of the twenty second century after *Rhapsody In Blue*, then some stuff they played in the middle of the twentieth century. The greats; Cash, Hooker, King, Vaughn, Nelson, Clapton, Page, Hendrix... I love classical guitar!

After *Rhapsody* played, more bubble gum music came on. I got another beer. The three guys playing pool left and a couple of college kids came in.

Rap City started playing. Good! I hate bubble gum music, and Chartov was a fantastic guitarist. It's too bad they executed him for sedition when he was only thirty. Too bad half the world's governments outlawed all his music for sixty years, too. He's still reviled in Russia to this day.

It's sad. Politics is nuts.

A lot of the guys I was playing died young, but most of them died from being young, wild, and stupid. Well, maybe Chartov died from being stupid, too, especially since the change he was singing about wanting didn't happen until half a century after he was dead. His music didn't do anything to change things, but change was ready when it was ready.

Huh? No, I ain't went to college but I like music.

Anyway, I drank three more beers and called a cab home. What? They were Newcastle, I told you, ain't you guys paying attention? I got home, took the lift to Ol' Miss and carried all the beer in. It hadn't all fit in the gantry, they'd left more than two thirds of it outside. After the five trips up the lift carrying all that beer to my boat I sat on the couch and opened one of them.

Huh? Another Newcastle, and no, I don't know what kind, the beer didn't come in bottles, it came in cans. It's funny, that's not the brand I usually drink but I was thinking about the hookers I was going to be hauling and an old classical song had popped into my head; it goes "Newcastle brown, it'll really smack you down, take a greasy whore and a rollin' dance floor..."

I woke up sitting on the couch with the doorbell screaming at me and a full warm flat beer on the table next to me. What damned time is it? Five? *In the God damned morning?* What the hell? I picked up my tablet. "Who is it and what in the hell do you want at this ungodly hour?" I growled.

"Tamatha Winters, who are you?" the woman pictured on the tablet said.

"I'm the captain of this damned boat. What in the hell do you want?"

"I'm part of your cargo."

"Christ, woman," I said, still irritated but noting that she wasn't bad looking. "We don't leave until Monday and it's only Saturday. At five o'clock in the God damned morning! Damn it, woman, I wanted to sleep late!"

"I'm sorry, but I don't have anywhere else to go," she said.

So I'm perplexed again. Or still. Or something. No place to go? A decent looking hooker? She's planning to sleep in her harness? "So why not?" I asked.

"Drops."

"Shit, an addict?"

"Yeah," the picture of the woman on the tablet said. "I heard there ain't no drops on Mars and I'm sick of the life. You think I *like* sucking dicks for... well, it ain't a living. More like a dying. I can't seem to stop on Earth, and they want women on Mars so I'm going."

"They don't want women, they want whores. You're still going to be a whore."

"Maybe," she said. "We'll see. Are you going to let me in?"

"I have to check the roster to see if you're authorized."

"Why? Isn't it your ship?"

"Look, lady," I said, "it's the company's ship. I just live here and drive it where they tell me to. I can't let you on unless I have you on the manifest. Let me look." I looked, there wasn't any Tamatha Winters or record of her face. "Sorry, lady, you ain't on the list."

"What?!" She said. "Of course I am! Here's my papers," she said, holding out a fone at the gantry camera.

"Sorry, lady," I said. "You'll have to straighten it out with the company. Bye."

"Wait!" the tablet exclaimed. "I can't go home! There's drops there and I won't make the liftoff!"

"Sorry, lady, I ain't gonna screw up a good job. I can actually buy shit instead of having crappy printed out shit and I ain't gonna mess it up. Good BYE!" I said, disconnected, and went to bed. At least the cunt had me in more comfortable sleep, my couch sucks to sleep on.

I didn't know she was lying. About everything.

Chapter Four

Destiny

The maid woke me up about noon. I hate that God damned maid, always noisy as hell. Why does it have to clean at noon? Those things should wait until people are awake, it ain't every day you can sleep late. I was going to have to be getting up at seven thirty every day in a few days and I wanted to sleep late, damn it! And I had to pay for the damned thing and my other personal robots, bought from the company because it was in my damned purchase contract for the houseboat. And they were damned expensive, I'll tell you. Each of them cost me an arm and a leg.

"Coffee," I growled. I especially hated paying for *that* damned robot. A couple of minutes later a table with a cup of coffee on it rolled up to me. Why are those damned things so slow? Anyway, I don't know why I'm putting this in my report except I don't want to get anybody killed just because I left anything out.

I took a shit and drank another cup of coffee. Damn but the robots make shitty coffee, I really hated paying for that robot. It cost me a lot of money and it really sucks at what it does. I should just make the coffee myself, this robot shit sucks.

At least the robots get free repairs and software upgrades and I get to keep it anywhere I want, and take it with me when I retire, I own it. Upgrades are supposed to be for life, which is why my robots cost me so much, I guess. Well, and probably because their employees are a captive audience. The company makes them for really cheap, they don't cost much at all to manufacture. I'll bet they don't sell many coffeebots to people who don't work for the company!

I switched on the video and turned to the news. Tornadoes, hurricanes, floods, fires, shootings, robberies, political corruption, some bullshit about the Martian terraforming project that's been going on for a hundred years... why do they call it "news"? It's never new, it's the same old shit all the time. Bored, I switched through all of the channels. Shit, all boring.

Later on I figured I'll get a beer somewhere where there's people. If I was lucky they wouldn't be boring people like all the boring people on the video. So I locked up Ol' Miss and hailed a taxi with my fone and went to the nearest bar, which was five miles away. Why ain't there no bars near spaceports, I wondered again. It was like that everywhere. I paid the cab fare and went inside and cussed myself; I forgot how expensive this damned place was and should have gone someplace cheaper. But at least there was a decent crowd here tonight, and some good classical music somebody else played was coming from the jukebox.

Huh? I don't remember, Presley, maybe. Yeah, come to think of it it was Presley but I don't know the name of the song. Something about shoes, I think.

I sat down and ordered a beer. "I'm sorry, sir," the bartender said, "but this says you're underage."

"What? Christ, lady, I'm forty five!"

"Well, this says 'underage, no ID carried'."

"Shit," I said, and got out my fone and turned on GPSID. "Try it again."

"Okay," she said, "It worked that time." I checked my balance – wow, beer was even more expensive here than I remembered. Well, I guess I didn't remember at all or I'd have gone to a different bar. I drank a Heineken tonight but was switching to some Australian beer because they were cheaper and damn but beer was expensive in this place. I should have stayed with Newcastle, that's what I had shipped to my boat.

"Hi, Captain."

"Huh?" I blurted out, startled. "Oh," I said, seeing who it was. "The woman that wanted on my boat. Gonna buy me a drink and try and get on my boat again, lady?"

"The name's Tamatha. You can call me Tammy. If I buy you a drink are you going to let me on?"

"Nope."

"How about a blow job?"

It was so absurd I laughed until my sides ached. There were going to be two hundred whores just like her on my boat. "You have *got* to be kidding me!" I said, still laughing. I thought, no wonder they have droppers in comedy movies, this was hilarious. Funnier than the movies, even.

"Buy your own booze, loser."

"Fuck you," I retorted, still chuckling. "I ain't cheap like you droppers. I can afford my own beer."

"I told you, I want to get away from that shit. That's why I haven't gone home, even though I really, really want to. Come on, please, I'll fuck you all the way to Mars!"

I laughed even harder. "Yeah, you and two hundred other hookers," I said, chuckling again.

"You're an asshole," she said.

"So what, cunt," I replied. "Get outta my face."

"What did you call me?" she demanded.

"Are you good for anything but putting a dick in?" I asked.

"OOOOH!!" She shouted, and stomped off. I got another expensive beer. Damn, I should have had the taxi take me to a cheaper part of town, even if the fare would have been more. I guess I could have took the bus, but hell, I got money, I don't need no damned bus.

A really good looking blonde sat down next to me. "Hi," she said. "I overheard, why did she call you Captain? Are you on the Mars boat?"

"Yeah," I said. "Why?"

"I'm going to Mars."

"Yeah? That's what she said. She's not on the manifest."

"I am."

"Yeah?" I said, pulling out my fone and checking out the manifest. Of course, as soon as I turned it on her face and information was shown. "Why, pleased to meet you, uh..." I glanced at the manifest, "Destiny? Is that your real name?"

She giggled. "Yeah, it is. My parents wanted me to have an uncommon first name because our last name is so common. Buy you a drink, Captain?"

"Call me John," I said, shaking her extended hand. "So why do you want to go to Mars?"

"I want to see what it's like to be a hooker."

I choked on my beer; women kind of fuck my brain up sometimes. "Huh?"

"I want to experience everything!"

She grabbed my crotch. "No charge for you," she said before locking lips with me.

Wow. I was really looking forward to this trip!

Ol' Miss, my boat, is really a houseboat. I'd kind of lied to that Tammy woman, my houseboat is my boat even though the gantry and the boosters and the harness tube belong to the company, but passengers don't ride in my boat, they ride in the tube. I usually only live in it when I'm on-planet; it won't go farther than the moon in any reasonable amount of time, and I live in the company's captain's quarters when I'm working. Lots nicer and bigger than my houseboat. The company pays me to ferry passengers to the ship, in orbit, then usually take them to wherever they're going after we dock. A second stage to hold a couple hundred passengers or a load of cargo is pretty cheap, it's just a tube, and if I'm hauling passengers it has gravity harnesses installed. Someone else usually ferries passengers and cargo out of orbit when we get where we're going, and I take Ol' Miss down.

I had a wonderful time! I really liked Destiny. Smart, funny, and *damned* good looking. I bought her drinks all night.

We shared a taxi to my boat, and she remarked that

cabs used to have drivers. She'd been fascinating me all night with tidbits of history and laughed at all my jokes. God but I liked this woman!

"What's a 'driver'?" I asked. Screwdrivers?

"They had automobiles for over a century and a half before they had computers or robots. They needed a human to steer it and use the throttle and brakes, all that. The person controlling the car was the car's driver. People used to get paid to drive cabs." Oh, that kind of driver.

The cab pulled up by the gantry and there were twenty women waiting there. I had to check them all in. "Sorry, Destiny," I said. "You can wait in my quarters until I'm done here."

"No," she said, and winked. "You can come to mine when you're done."

"Uh, your quarters are in orbit," I said. "This isn't the ship, this is just a rocket underneath a harness tube underneath my houseboat. The ship itself is in orbit waiting for us. Just take the gantry lift to my boat and when we take off you can use a harness there, you don't have to ride in the tube. You can leave your stuff in my boat until we dock, they don't give you much room for belongings in the tube anyway, not near enough for your three suitcases."

Huh? So what if she was cargo. So was my beer but I carry that, my boat was half full of it. I never said nobody but me ever rides my boat. Fuck you two assholes. You want me to leave right now? Then shut the fuck up.

The fucking women just wouldn't stop coming, and most of them acted horny, a sure sign they were high on drops. Most of them hit on me, none too subtly. And they had weird eyes, with one pupil bigger than the other, just like in those silly comedies.

This was going to be a good trip! At least, if I could get all those whores inside the boat. No sooner than I'd start walking to the gantry lift to go home than the damned bell rang with another one walking up to the gate. It kept up all weekend. Finally, maybe midnight Sunday, I got what I thought was going to be eight hours sleep. I'd had maybe four all weekend.

I fell asleep in the chair after letting the last one in and got two more hours sleep before the bell rang again. It was that damned Tammy woman. "You ain't getting in," I said. "Now go away before I call the cops."

"Check your manifest."

I checked it. "You aren't on it."

"Look at the passengers list."

Passengers? Huh? Passenger tickets were expensive. But okay, I checked. Damn, she was there, business class, no less. Where did a whore get the money for a normal trip to Mars, let alone the money for a business class ticket? I unlocked the gantry lift to the tube's airlock. "Harness seventeen," I said, and went to my cabin. Okay, fuck you, houseboat. You guys trying to piss me off?

I got some sleep, finally... an hour later.

I finally had some time alone with Destiny. I *really* like Destiny!

Chapter Five

Liftoff

I woke up to the smell of bacon and coffee and the sound of a woman saying "Good morning, Johnny."

It took me a second or two to figure out who was talking because I was a little hungover. "Mmmh," I said. "Mornin', Destiny." I got lucky, I usually suck at remembering names, but hers was so different it was easy.

"Come have some eggs before they get cold, John."

"You made breakfast? Damn, I think I'm in love!"

She laughed. "Slow down, cowboy. And no, the robot made breakfast. I only made the coffee."

I took a sip. It was really good coffee! But I'd been drinking that nasty robot crap. I laughed with her. "Don't worry, I'm a snail. I thought you liked me too?"

She grinned sheepishly. "I do. That's the problem. I didn't want to like you, I wanted to use you. But I can't, I like you too much.

"I might even be falling in love, damn it. Shit, I shouldn't have said that."

I was glad she did. I thought I was falling in love, too. Something just clicked with us, it seemed. Never happened before, I don't know why I married my ex. But I might be...

My brain exploded again.

It was a little awkward but I had a way out. I sighed. "Time to secure the passenger and cargo for liftoff. I guess you're first, lover."

Her eyes twinkled. "Lover?"

"No?"

She smiled. "Yeah."

Strapping and unstrapping is easy but you have to know how to do it, so you needed help the first time. I strapped her into a houseboat harness and started on the other two hundred women in the tube. Okay, one hundred ninety nine, sheesh. All of them looked happy but nervous. And horny. And all of them with their weird eyes with one pupil bigger than the other. When I finished strapping them all in I strapped myself into the houseboat's pilot chair and waited.

I hate liftoff. I wish I could just ride my houseboat up without the damned rocket boosters, I hate having her go through all that stress, let alone taking the gravities myself, but somebody has to be harnessed in the pilot seat and they have to be trained.

I wished this was a first class trip. They fly first class passengers up in a space plane to the lower edge of the atmosphere or something, then a liquid-fueled rocket on the space plane takes over and gradually adds thrust until it's at escape velocity. It isn't uncomfortable at all, but it's damned expensive, and slow. Rockets from the ground, now, those aren't the least bit comfortable but they're whole lot faster and a whole lot cheaper.

The countdown finally reached T minus ten.

"Ten... Nine... Eight... Seven... Six... Five... Four... Three... Two..."

I braced myself for the Gs. It isn't like riding ions like when you travel between planets, they use chemical rockets to get in orbit. They say it's because chemical rockets are cheaper for that, it's one reason that only people who can afford to buy judges can afford a first class ticket. There's a lot of gravities when the rocket lifts off. Looking back, the whores probably enjoyed liftoff.

I gripped the G harness and closed my eyes tight.

"...One. Ignition. Liftoff."

God but I hate liftoff. Hey, you wanted this report to be complete, didn't you? Then shut the fuck up and let me talk.

21

Jesus, guys.

Anyway, after we were in orbit I docked the tube on the port side of the ship, then I undocked my houseboat from the tube and docked it to the ship's pilot room dock. Once inside the pilot room I raised the generators to full power and slowly started accelerating, and the ship started moving; unharnessing is easier with gravity. Almost everything is easier with gravity. Except maybe gymnastics.

I went back in the houseboat to help Destiny get out of her harness, since it's almost impossible if nobody shows you how. We went into the ship, walked to the docking bay, and Destiny helped me unleash the rest. In fact, most of the rest helped unleashed the rest and it went a hell of a lot faster than it did to strap them in, faster than I expected. I was impressed, maybe the whores weren't as depraved as I thought?

It turned out that that I was completely wrong. They were more depraved than I could imagine.

I was carrying dangerous animals and didn't know it. In fact, they were monsters.

Chapter Six

Catfight

The tube stayed connected to the rocket to get it back to Earth. Well, not all the way, the rocket jettisons the tube and the tube burns up from friction with the atmosphere and then the rocket lands by computer control for refueling and maintenance.

Three days after we had lifted off, gone into orbit and docked with the ship, quarters had been assigned to the women, the rocket went back down on autopilot, the tube was, as the egghead science nerds say, "jettisoned in a trajectory" that would burn it up; they say it's supposed to be cheaper than landing them, and we were on our way to Mars.

Mars, Ho!

There's nothing I could add that ain't in the logs or what I've been rambling on about for the last three hours, nothing happened on the engine or generator inspections, not even robots working on any of them, and of course my eight o'clock course adjustments didn't need any adjusting, I just checked the readouts. They were all normal, expected, of course, at the first of any journey.

I was watching a movie, Destiny cuddled in my arm. God, but I liked this woman. She was like a female me, only refined, she'd went to college. Hell, she had a doctorate in astronomy. My woman was a scientist! Man, life was sure good.

Of course, the tablet had to ruin the mood, damn it. I had to go to the commons area.

Right now the commons area was a bar and the robots summoned me because there was a damned bar fight. Shit.

I like having company but I hate being a babysitter.

Tables were overturned, two women were fist fighting so I tasered and handcuffed both of the dumbasses. "Okay," I said, "Who are you girls and what's this all about?" I noticed that unlike when we left orbit their eyes looked normal.

"I'm Billie and that bitch called me a cunt so I hit her," the blonde with the black eye said.

"I'm Sparkle," the other one said. "And I was just defending myself from that cunt."

I sighed. "Look, bitches, there ain't gonna be no violence on my boat, get it? Billie, you're confined to quarters, and that means the door's locked, for twenty four hours. It happens again and you're locked up for the rest of the trip. Got it? That shit just don't happen on my boat.

"Sparkle, you get two hours and you better stay out of trouble." I escorted them to their quarters and removed their handcuffs, locked the doors and told the computer how long to keep them locked up, and returned to Destiny.

If I'd went to college maybe I'd known about drops. You sure don't learn about them from watching comedies, I'd find out later.

As I was going back to my quarters, Tammy walked up. Tammy, my sole passenger. Another dropper. Where in the hell did she get the money for a ticket, I wondered again. Probably stole it, I guessed. "Trouble?" She asked.

"Nope, just a couple of pissed off whores," I said. Yeah, I held this woman in contempt. A dropper whore was... well, you don't want to know one. Believe me.

"That's what happens when they don't get their drops," she said.

"Huh?" I hadn't known whores or droppers, but I knew I didn't want to.

"Droppers get violent when they don't get their drops."
"You?"
"Best not fuck with me, asshole."
Shit, no wonder the company gave me a raise. Droppers

and no drops.

I was in trouble.

Or maybe not. It was half a week before another such incident occurred, and was quickly quelled; I didn't have to ground the kids this time.

When I say "babysitter" I'm not kidding. These fully grown women acted like spoiled children. It's like they weren't raised right, I don't know.

Hey, can I go to the bathroom? Thanks.

Okay, where was I? Oh, yeah, drops.

I knew those damned things were addictive, but I didn't know that withdrawal from them caused violence. And not just fistfights, but deadly violence. Terrible, horrible, inhuman, unthinkable violence. And, it seemed, every time. I was in deep trouble and didn't know it.

Chapter Seven

Drops

I'd been with Destiny for a week and a half now and it seems like that long that I've been talking into this thing. Is anybody actually going to read all this? I mean, I told you when I got up and what I ate and drank and what everybody said and what we watched for every damned day. Yeah, you're right, as long as they pay me but I'm doing great these days. I'm retiring as soon as I get done with this report and I'm going to open a bar here.

Anyway, Destiny and me was talking about how fewer and fewer droppers were wearing clothes over scrambled eggs and bacon and coffee before I had to go to work. Yeah, my job is work. Only the first week is easy, usually. I have to go to the pilot room and make sure we weren't going the wrong way, then I usually have to inspect the whole ship, and I have a pretty big boat. You think the people part is big? It's tiny compared to the rest of the ship. Yeah, the passenger cabins are like good sized apartments and the cargo pens are big, but storage, tools, robots and other machinery takes up ninety percent of boats. Hell, storage takes a lot more space than passenger quarters and cargo pens combined, including the sick bay and commons. The engines are about five stories high; at least, judging from all the God damned stairs I have to go down on inspections. Five damned flights of them.

And I had to inspect all of it except the occupied passenger quarters, and I only had one passenger. The machinery is every damned day, and sometimes twice if I find anything that's broke. Except cargo pens and passenger quarters, upstairs is only twice a week. It's a lot of walking, believe me. Even though we only have three quarters gravity; we get the gravity from acceleration. When we get more than halfway there I'll turn the boat around and we'll have zero gravity until we get turned around, but that only takes a few minutes.

I'll have to inspect it twice that day. Something always seems to break when you turn them around, but it's almost always something simple and the robots can usually fix it pretty fast and easy. It usually looks to me like they're engineering this junk to be cheap. Stupid bean counters, if they used better parts repairs wouldn't cost the company so much. The fools are penny wise and dollar foolish, probably all of them know the price of everything and the value of nothing.

Anyway, I asked Destiny if she was really going to be a hooker. She giggled, and said "You're not going to turn me in to the company, are you?"

Shit. "Uh, what? I mean, turn you in for what?"

"You'll keep it a secret? If you can't we're done."

Shit Shit Shit Shit Shit.

"Yeah." Sweat was running down my cheek.

"Okay, John, I have no intention of becoming a hooker. I just signed up because it was the cheapest way to get to Mars."

"But your contract..."

"Cheaper to break than buying passage. I have a pretty good lawyer, John. She's also a really good friend that I went to college with and she teaches me stuff."

"Well, okay," I said. "As long as nobody knows, I don't know. I Kind of wished you hadn't told me."

"I don't want to keep secrets from you, John. I think I'm in love."

"Lets get married!" I was certain I wanted to spend my life with her.

"Lets take it a little slower, okay, John?"

"I guess," I said. "I'd better go to work."

"See you, lover," she said, kissing me. God but I liked

this woman.

The pilot room was close to the captain's quarters, of course. Hah! Captain! My crew was a bunch of computers and robots and other machines, I only had one passenger and the passenger and my cargo was whores.

Shit. Some "captain" I was. Captain Hooker and two hundred peter panhandlers.

While I was walking through the boat I heard cats fighting. What the hell? There weren't supposed to be any cats in my boat, but it sounded like two of them were in here fighting. I ran toward the sound, which was coming from the Commons.

It wasn't cats. It was Lek and Lek, two whores from Thailand. There were three Thais on board but the third pretty much kept to herself, I didn't see much of the other one. Lek could talk English okay but Lek only spoke a little pidgin English and not very much at that, almost none.

Wouldn't you know it, two people from the same country with the same names. I couldn't pronounce either of their last names. And they were in the throes of violence – Lek punched Lek so hard she flew all the way across the room and bounced off of a wall. It was like some of the ancient twentieth century kung-fu movies me and Destiny like to watch sometimes. Of course, those movies were silly and the boat's at low gravity. So it looked really silly when that whore knocked the other whore across the room like in one of those stupid old movies. I laughed my ass off.

I'd talked to Lek before, the one who spoke English pretty good, or at least good enough that you could understand her. It seems that in Thailand, prostitutes are revered for their service to humanity. I'm sure all those horny nerds on Mars will agree wholeheartedly.

I think she's full of shit.

"Okay," I said, "What the hell is this all about?"

"I don't know," said the semi-fluent one. "She just attacked me!"

"Coon me drops! My me drops! Meow drops!" the other one babbled. At least, that's what it sounded like she said. It was weird, the words almost sounded like English but they made no sense the way they were strung together.

"She think I have drops and she want some. I guess she out of 'em."

Uh, Oh. "There are drops on my boat?"

"Are you stupid? Yes. Everybody got them."

"You?"

She laughed. "Come find 'em," she said with that twinkle in her eyes with different sized pupils that, well, I saw in most of them when they boarded. Droppers' eyes almost always looked weird, with one pupil big and one small, but I hadn't seen them at their weirdest yet, when they were going through withdrawal. They're downright terrifying then.

I gave the less fluent Lek an hour of confinement, noticing that her eyes looked normal, except that they were a little bloodshot. Kids, you gotta ground 'em sometimes. I didn't have a clue what to do about the drops. I should have went to college.

I went down the five damned flights of stairs and inspected the engines and the generators... shit, I had no idea how they worked but I was supposed to inspect them? Okay, just follow the checklist on my tablet and I don't have to have a clue.

A robot was working on one, the first time this trip a robot was working on an engine. I noted it in the ship's log, which is standard procedure. Even though there's always a robot working on one after the first week or so in space, seems like.

I was still chuckling about the Thai chick flying across the room in the boat's reduced gravity. We could do better than one G but the bean counters say it would cost too much, so I fly 'em like they tell me to, even though it seems stupid to me, because fusion fuel is dirt cheap and lasts forever. Maybe it's got something to do with maintenance, I don't think they covered that in training. Times like that I'm glad gravity is reduced, that was hilarious!

See, they tell me the gravity is from propulsion, we're always burning fuel. Or acceleration or something, I ain't never went to college.

I stopped by the houseboat and got a bottle of wine, and walked back to our quarters. I opened the door – and saw her with an eyedropper.

SHIT!!! Destiny was a dropper!

Chapter Eight

Confession

I was so startled I almost dropped the bottle. "Destiny! Oh no! Oh my God, no! Not you!"

"Huh?" she said with a concerned look on her face. "What's wrong, John?"

"What's wrong? Jesus Christ! You're a dropper! Oh, God..." I was devastated.

She looked at the eyedropper and laughed. "These aren't angel tears, silly, they're antibiotics."

"Antibiotics? What, you got pinkeye?"

She laughed again. "Don't worry, I don't have any diseases. I had the lenses in my eyes replaced with implants a couple of weeks before we left. I have to put these drops in my eyes once a week for another month. It was three times a day for the first week and once a day for the next week. It's just to prevent infection."

"Why did you have to get Implants?" I asked.

"I was nearsighted, my vision was twenty forty and I had a little astigmatism, too. These new lenses are great, they're like having strong binoculars and a built in microscope. I never would have believed how sharp and clear everything would be. I can see a blood cell, and the doctor said I should be able to see Earth's moon or Saturn's rings from Mars if the planets' orbits are in the right places. It's perfect for an astronomer! An astronomer's eyes are one of astronomy's best tools."

"Wow. Did it hurt?"

"Did what hurt?"

"The surgery."

"No, it's painless. You don't feel a thing."

"Still," I said, "I'd have just worn contacts rather than let somebody stick needles in my eyes."

"Well, I used to wear them but they said they'd get in the way on Mars. And I can see so good now! I'm really glad I had the procedure."

Procedure. Folks who went to college talk like that. I thought of something... "You told me once you were planning on taking advantage of me. How and why?"

"Oh, John, you're going to hate me."

"Well, look, you already confessed."

She sighed. "I lied to you, I work for the organization that hired your company. My job was supposed to be keeping the whores from taking over your ship. But I didn't expect to like you so much. Actually, I didn't expect to like you at all. They told me you were an asshole."

I laughed. "I am an asshole! It's part of my job."

"Is that for me?" she said, looking at the wine.

"It's for us. Got a corkscrew and glasses?"

"Robot, open this wine," she said. A square box with rounded corners wheeled across the room with two wine glasses sitting on top of it. I set the bottle on it and grippers grabbed the bottle while a corkscrew came out on an arm with hinges... oh, hell, you've seen boat robots, sorry. What? You haven't? Why in the hell did they send you two? Anyway, the thing opened and poured the wine. I started to take a sip.

"You have to let it breathe," she said.

"I gotta what?" I asked.

She laughed. "Let it sit for a couple of minutes. It'll taste better."

I asked why and she gave me a complicated answer that I didn't understand that had something to do with chemistry. At least, I think she was talking about chemistry. I should have went to college.

"You never did tell me why you were going to Mars," I

said.

"I just told you, I work for the company."

"Yeah, but if you were only going to be on Mars for a week or so your contact lenses wouldn't have been much of a hassle. So you must be planning on staying."

"I am, yeah. I just took the job on your boat to earn a little beer money and passage to Mars, not that I need money but I'm obsessively frugal by nature. I told you I had a PhD, and that I'm an astronomer. Well, there are too many photons produced on Earth..."

"Whoa, slow down," I said. "I ain't went to college and ain't got a clue what you're talking about. What are 'photons'?"

"Photons are what light and radio waves are made of. It's way too bright everywhere on Earth for astronomy and there hasn't been a useful telescope on the planet for well over a century. So it was the moon or Mars, and they have plenty of people on the moon. Mars isn't just short of women, it's short of everything and everybody. Almost everyone there is a scientist; there's no unemployment on Mars at all. It needs more robots, too. It needs more of everything. It's a real frontier, I think it's really exciting, like an adventure."

Adventure? It was old hat to me. I'd made the Mars trip lots of times. Now Saturn, that was an adventure. I'd been on my way back from Titan one trip and the damned engines quit and the robots couldn't fix them any more than they can perk decent coffee, although they can fix most stuff most of the time. But not that time. I had to wait six damned months for a tow tug and I'd made it half way home when the boat crapped out on me. It took six months because it was a rush job and I was at a full gravity and about to turn around when they went out, so I was way off course by the time the tug got to me.

Mars was usually a two or three week trip, but it was on the opposite side of the sun and we were going to be in space for a couple of months. I have no idea why the company didn't just wait two weeks or maybe not even that long to launch, we'd have gotten there a lot sooner but what the hell, I do what they tell me to do and they pay me to do it. But that's a long time to put up with dropless whores.

Destiny raised her glass. "To Mars!" she said.

"Nah," I replied. "To us."

She smiled. "I'll drink to that! Are you staying on Mars with me?"

An alarm went off. It never fails. I grabbed my tablet.

Shit! A fire! In space, a fire is the last damned thing you need. Well, almost. But bad just the same.

Chapter Nine

Finance

The CEO of the company was annoyed. More than annoyed. He put the report down and buzzed his secretary.

"Yes sir?" she said.

"Who's in charge of scheduling?"

"I believe that's Ms. Martinez."

"She's in charge that department?"

"Yes, sir."

"I want to see her. Right now."

"Yes sir."

"I want to see Larry Griffins, too. I want both of them here immediately."

"Yes sir."

He drummed his fingers as he waited impatiently for his incompetent staff. This was inexcusable, so they damned well better have a good excuse. The two finally came in together with worried looks on their faces; neither had actually met the highest ranking officer in the company, although the head of financial had spoken with him on the fone a few times, and the CEO had an angry look on his face.

He said said "Miss Martinez..."

"Missus," she said defiantly. She was going to get fired anyway, she thought, even though she didn't know why. If she were going to get fired, she'd not be disrespected.

"Sorry, *Missus* Martinez," the CEO answered sarcastically. "I'd like to know why Mars two eighty four didn't wait a week and a half to launch. And you, Mister Griffins, why are you letting stockholders' money be wasted like that?"

Both looked puzzled, and said in unison "Sir?" Martinez added "I don't understand. We schedule according to launch booster availability as the requests come in, in order. Rush jobs are first in line."

"And you allow this, Griffins?"

"I'm sorry, sir, I don't understand, either."

"Christ!" Green exclaimed, exasperated. "Didn't either of you two go to college?"

"Yes sir, I went to U of I," Martinez said.

"I have an MBA from..." Griffins started.

Green interrupted him. "It's basic physics, people! Orbital mechanics! My boat captains think you're really ignorant, they know how stupid it is to launch at the wrong time and are reporting on it, and they're only high school graduates who probably can't even do algebra."

Martinez frowned. "I only had one physics class, my major was math."

Green shook his head. "Look, you two need to communicate better with the other departments. Especially you, Mr. Griffins.

"Mrs. Martinez, we have astrophysicists who could save this company a lot of money if you'd let them. Don't just have them plot trajectories, talk to them and even more importantly listen to them. Don't just have them guide ships, I want them to guide how you do what you do and more importantly, when. If that ship had waited a week and a half before leaving, it would have gotten there much sooner. We're paying for food and fuel and this is a tremendous waste, not to mention a great inconvenience for our paying clients.

"Griffins, this is mostly on you. You're supposed to be finding ways to save this company money and undereducated boat captains are doing a better job of it than you are. I have reports that we're underenginnering parts to save money, and spending even more to replace them. Don't issue orders to engineering; you're not an engineer. Listen to them, make sure you find out repair costs and calculate that in with engineering and manufacturing costs, you should have learned that when you got your business degree. Let engineering decide how strong the parts need to be, that's why they hold engineering degrees.

"Martinez, from now on consult with astrophysics for scheduling! Make sure that rush orders will get there as fast as possible, not launch as fast as possible. Travelers or animal cargo should be scheduled so they're on the ship the shortest amount of time unless there's a rush job in front of it, because we have to feed them, and the pork on our first class flights is incredibly expensive and none of the food or animal feed is free. Astrophysics can figure this stuff out, talk to them. Listen to them. You should already be doing it. Now get back to work, both of you."

They left and he buzzed his secretary. "I want a meeting with all department heads tomorrow at nine in the morning." These people were going to communicate with each other or he'd replace them all.

"Yes, sir. Mister Bush is on vacation in Rio though, sir."

"Then have whoever he left in charge attend and contact Bush and tell him he'd damned well better be there by teleconference, and I don't care if he's on the beach in South America naked with a tablet."

"Yes sir," she said. "Wow," she thought, "he's really in a bad mood today!"

He picked up his tablet and started reading again.

Chapter Ten

Fire!

"Shit!" I yelled. "A fire! Son of a bitch!"

I took off running toward the burning quarters that the alarm was screaming from and I heard a human screaming as I approached the door. Horrible, blood-curdling screams of terrible, excruciating pain and fear. And then, even worse than the screaming, the human screams abruptly stopped while the alarm screamed on.

The light above the door was flashing red. Solid red meant you could only open it from the inside unless you were captain, solid yellow meant go in but don't come out. You guys know, if there's a flashing red light on your door you need to get the hell out of there *right then* before it stops flashing. The alarm kept screaming but whoever was in there had stopped screaming, and all of the doors' lights were solid yellow, meaning come in and stay in, except the one flashing red.

When a door flashed red on the outside it was solid red on the inside and nobody but me could get it open from either side.

The door wouldn't open, even for me. I was horrified and I may even have panicked a little. "Computer," I said to the tablet. "Open that God damned door, there's someone in there that's hurt!"

"Unable to comply," it said.

"Reason?"

"Danger to the ship and passenger, other cargo, and crew."

"GOD DAMN IT!" I yelled. "There's a woman dying in

there. God damned computer!"

"Containment in approximately two minutes." This must be a bad one for the automatic fire suppression to take that long to take hold – but of course, since the cabin was occupied it couldn't just let all the air out like if one of the engine rooms had caught fire, or a maid or other robot caught fire in an unoccupied room.

"OPEN THAT GODDAMNED DOOR!" I screamed at the tablet.

"Unable to comply" the computer answered emotionlessly again. God damned piece of shit computer! God DAMN it! There was a human being in there and I didn't care how she made her money, she was a *person*.

I think I changed my mind about hookers then. I kind of pitied them.

Three of the whores showed up wondering what was going on. I ignored them and continued stupidly and uselessly screaming at the tablet. "God damn it computer, I'm going to..."

Yeah, getting emotional with a computer and threatening it is pretty damned stupid but I'd kind of lost it. The whores were all yammering and I kept ignoring them and kept uselessly yelling at the damned stupid computer like I was a witless idiot.

A medic rolled up behind me and the door opened, air rushing into the smoke-filled quarters, its pressure already lowered but not enough to harm a person.

Huh? What the hell? You don't know what a medic is? Medics are robots that look kind of like narrow tables with padded tops and appendages to measure bodily functions and administer medicine and stuff like that. Planetside they call them "gurneys" but everything is named different on a boat, which you two guys obviously ain't never been on. Like port and starboard. Which makes no sense with a space ship, because the portholes are all on the ceilings and that's the only place you can see stars, and the ceiling is the bow. And the deck faces the stern.

God but it stunk when I walked into the room! A burned flesh smell and a burned chemical smell. A nasty burned chemical, even making the burned flesh smell smell worse, if you can believe that. It was even worse.

It was no wonder the computer wouldn't open the door, I'd have been cooked as done as the woman, and the other three women, too. Hell, as bad as it looked the whole damned boat might have gone up in flames.

The medic lifted the woman, who I recognized as the Billie whore, on itself. I recognized her, but barely. She was burned up pretty bad, real bad. The medic robot, which was the table, put an oxygen mask over her face and a needle in her arm and sprayed her with water, and the cot and her left for the sick bay.

"Damn it, Joe," one of the women said, "What's wrong with Billie? What happened?"

"I don't know, there was a fire," I replied. "I'm investigating so stay the hell out of my way."

Another one said "She's been trying to bum drops from everybody. Probably trying to cook up some other drug."

I walked around the smoky room and saw what caused the fire – the stupid whore was indeed trying to make an ancient drug called "methamphetamine". Even on Earth making that shit is dangerous if you're not a chemist that's went to college, in space it's a fucking crazy menace. I guessed that since she couldn't get angel tears she figured she'd make a substitute, as if all drugs were alike or something. Dumb whore. It was just crazy.

My fone buzzed; it was Destiny. "Is everything okay?"

"Yeah, sugar, just one of those stupid whores trying to get high. Blew up her quarters and burned herself up pretty good."

I went outside. As soon as I did the door closed and I could hear the windy sound of smoky air being blown out to space. I wondered why they wasted it like that? Cheaper than filtering, I guess.

A maid was already waiting outside the door to clean up the mess and I started walking back home. A dozen whores were coming down the hallway towards me. "What's going on?"

"Billie blew herself up trying to make drugs," I said. "I catch anybody else doing that and they're in deep shit. Now excuse me."

"Wait! Is she okay?"

It was that one broad, Sparkle, the one that was fighting with Billie the first week. Apparently they'd not only made up, but were lovers. Lesbian hookers? That don't make no sense to me, but I ain't went to college. The bunch of them went on to the sick bay and I went back to drink some wine with Destiny. The robots would take care of Billie.

As I walked back to my cabin I pulled out my fone and hailed the ship's public address system. "Attention, cargo and passenger," I said. "There has been a fire caused by someone really, really stupid. Pay attention, now. If I catch any open flames whatever, the lady with the fire is locked up 'til we get to Mars. So if you're going to try to make drugs, you damned well better not need fire to do it. And even if you don't use fire if I catch you with drugs you're alone until we get there. So be good."

As I passed the commons there were two naked women having oral sex with each other. "Hey, you two. Get a room," I growled. What the hell was wrong with these whores? Almost none of them seemed to be wearing clothes lately.

They ignored me.

"You wanna be locked up?"

"Fuck off, Joe."

"That's Captain Knolls to you," I said, and pulled out my taser.

"You're an asshole."

"Get. Both of you. You're alone the next twenty four hours."

They weren't paying me enough for this shit. Fucking droppers!

Well, Destiny would cheer me up, she always did. I was actually pretty cheerful when I got back.

"Took you long enough," she said slyly.

"Oh, them whores," I said. "I had to lock a couple of 'em up."

"What did they do?"

"They were having oral sex with each other in the commons. I told 'em to go somewhere more private and they told me to fuck off. Look, hon, there's two hundred of them and they act like feral children. They'll take over if I let 'em."

"Feral?" she grinned.

"You're rubbing off on me, Brainiac!"

She giggled. "Here, I got some cheese while you were gone."

I picked up my glass. "To cheese!"

She laughed. "I'll drink to that. Want to watch something?"

"Nah, put on some music and we'll cuddle."

"Cuddle?"

"Well, you know where cuddling always goes."

Chapter Eleven

Hangover

I woke up with the worst hangover I had in years. Damn that wine! I usually drank beer and I hadn't drank any of that at all in a week or so, and not more than two or three at a time even then.

I was miserable. I didn't want to get out of the spinning bed, but I really had to pee bad, real bad. I staggered into the head and peed like forever. I wanted coffee. Damn, I was going to have to make coffee, the robots suck at making coffee. I hate robot coffee. Fuck it, I'll put up with robot coffee.

I put on a robe and stumbled into the kitchen – and smelled coffee. *Good* coffee, not that robot crap. It took a few seconds for my hungover eyes that I hadn't really used since I woke up, and in fact maybe I was still asleep, to see Destiny and two cups of coffee at the table.

What a woman!

"You're not hung over?" I asked.

"Hung over? I'm still drunk," she said.

I sipped my coffee. "What time is it?"

The table, one of those damned new ones that talk, said "The present time is..."

"I wasn't talking to you, computer." I hate that table.

Destiny laughed. "I don't know what time it is. Tuesday, maybe?"

"Computer."

"Waiting for input."

Who programs these stupid things, anyway? "What damned time is it?"

"Please name the dam you want the present time for."

"Damn it, what time is it here and now?

"The present time on ship is seven fifty seven."

Shit, who programs... SHIT, I got three minutes to get to the pilot room.

"Shit!" I said. "I'm sorry, honey, I have to run."

"Shouldn't you put some pants on first?"

"I'm wearing a robe, I gotta go." I kissed her. "Bye." I ran to the pilot room, coffee mug in hand.

I got there with two minutes to spare. All the readouts said systems were nominal, which is egghead space talk for "everything is working right like it's supposed to be and it don't look like there's anything broke." At least, I think that's what it means.

I went back to my quarters, kissed Destiny, put on the clothes I wore the day before, filled my mug back up, and went on the morning inspection while little men with jackhammers were busy inside my head making my brain hurt.

The reduced gravity didn't make my head less light or my stomach less queasy.

I inspected the passengers' quarters first, since they were up front. Except Tammy's, of course. Passengers deserved privacy.

After the little incident with the explosion and fire I checked the cargo pens a little closer than I had been. Yeah, the doors to the store rooms, engines, and places they shouldn't be in stay locked but who knows what these drug addled whores know? For all I knew, one could be a locksmith. I couldn't even tell a whore from a real woman, look at Destiny, I thought she was a whore at first, just because she was cargo.

I'd billeted Destiny in the closest cargo quarters to my quarters, but it hadn't mattered since she'd only went there once after the takeoff. She's been in my quarters ever since.

This was the part I hated. I knocked on the door. Hell, I didn't have to since they were cargo but I don't want to be any more of an asshole than I have to be. In some situations you

44

have no choice, you got to be an asshole, but you don't have to like it.

I'm a boat captain, I'm used to being an asshole. I don't like it, but it's a shitty part of a great job. *Usually* a great job, this trip wasn't.

The voice on the other side of the door said "Who is it and what do you want? I ain't got no drops, bitch."

"It's Captain Knolls. I'm doing ship inspection. May I come in?"

"No. Fuck off, asshole."

"Door, open." The door opened and I went in. She was naked. The only one I'd seen wearing clothes for the last week was Tammy. "I don't have to be polite, dumbass. I just am. I'll skip it from now on if you prefer assholes."

"I ain't got no drops, bitch."

Gee, I've been hearing that a lot lately, and usually from one whore to another. "I ain't looking for drops. Just routine, damage or danger of damage."

"I ain't got no drops, bitch!"

"Whatever."

As I left for the next apartment... what? Yes, "apartment", these were civilian quarters, even though cargo pens were single room apartments. Anyway, as I was going out, two naked whores passed me, laughing. It was the two Thai chicks laughing about the fat blonde German hooker whose name I can never remember. Hell, there's two hundred of 'em and I ain't went to college or nothing and I ain't good with names in the first place. It sounded like they were making fun of the blonde, anyway. They were "talking" in fake German and saying "Nine! Nine! Nine!"

Like I said, lately it had got to where the only people on the boat who wore clothes were me, Destiny, and that Tammy girl. Must be the drops, I guessed.

Nobody else was home, except Kathy and Dawn, who just yelled "come in" when I rang the doorbell and kept on playing with each other's pussies while I did my inspection.

I'd skipped the sick bay and commons, I'd check them when I got back. They were between cargo and passenger quarters.

Then I walked down the five damned flights of stairs. It always smelled like ozone down there; those generators make a hell of a lot of electricity and the engines use what the generators feed them. Next was them and the engines, at the bottom of the stairs, and they never had anything wrong with them. Well, almost never, they all went out on me on my way back from that Titan run. They should keep them in a vacuum, I thought, because I never once found a problem during an inspection and it didn't keep the engines on that run from crapping out on me. Every damned one of 'em. All in a row, two at a time after the first one blew.

That Saturn run... that's why I stopped doing cargo. Lot of good my inspections did there. Jesus, that's a long time to be alone, I almost went crazy. I almost quit, but the company said I'd have passenger runs after that.

It isn't like the boat stops moving when the engines stop. It's worse. You keep going but have no way to maneuver, you just keep going at the speed you were when the engines stopped and you don't have any gravity at all and they have to come to you to tow you to port. It's a good thing the life support system isn't hooked in with the rest of the systems and has its own batteries.

I checked out all of the shit my tablet told me to check out and walked back to the sick bay. Next time I'm on Earth I'm getting a bicycle or something, this is a big damned boat. I'll still have five stories of stairs to climb, though. Maybe I'll get two bikes...

I walked into sick bay. "Hi, Billie," I said.

"Um, yeah, I am" she said, looking at the IV tube.

"Don't get too used to it, you won't be in here long."

"Well, I guess if I want to get high I'll hurt myself!"

"Nope, that's up to me. Next time it's naproxin."

While I was there I got some naproxin myself; my head

was still throbbing but my stomach had stopped doing gymnastics. Now to inspect the commons.

The commons area was huge, an eighth the size of the entire passengers and cargo decks with a fully automated kitchen, with robotic cooks and servers.

It was full of naked whores.

Half of them were practically begging me to have sex with them. Man, if it wasn't for Destiny I'd be having a hell of an orgy right now. I hurried my ass back to my quarters when the inspection was over as fast as I could.

Destiny was sleeping when I got out of the shower, so I figured I'd go over the inventory list. The maid would be noisy in about thirty minutes or so.

A while before the noisy damned machine showed up an alarm went off. Damn. DAMN! Fucking whores!

But this time it wasn't the whores, it was a distress call from another one of our company's ships. "Knolls, here," I said to the tablet. "How can I help?"

I didn't know how far away the other boat was but it would probably take at least a minute and probably longer for the signal to get to it unless it was really close. I laid the tablet down and opened a beer. Hair of the dog, you know. Halfway through the beer I decided to return the favor for Destiny; she was going to need coffee when she woke up, so I made a pot.

The rackety machine came in and started noisily cleaning. Destiny woke up. "Damn, that thing's noisy," she said. "Do I smell coffee?"

"Yeah," I said. "I started a pot for you. It's almost done."

When it finished perking I poured a cup and handed it to her, and sat down next to her. "Thanks," she said "What do you want to do today..."

The tablet interrupted her. "Captain Knolls? Is that you, John? Kelly here. Thank God somebody's in range. I'm about a minute and thirty light seconds behind you and one of my engines shorted out and blew both of my generators and drained all my batteries except life support. It didn't leave enough energy for me to make the Mars landing. I'm just coasting, so I'm going to be weeks late. Can you charge my batteries so I don't have to call for a tow, old buddy?"

Hey, it was Bill Kelly, an old friend driving one of our company boats. I'd known Kelly for years, went to high school with him when we were kids. "Wild Bill" they'd called him, even though he wasn't very wild at all. Actually, Bill's kind of a nerd, loves reading and tinkering. It caused him a few problems with the jocks in high school, who seemed to hate smart people in general and nerds in particular. But me and him were always real good friends.

"Hey, Bill, sorry about your luck," I answered. "Yeah, of course I can give you a jump, you might even have enough charge that you won't be too late. I'll slow this thing down for a while and change course so we can dock."

"Boat captains sure are busy," Destiny said.

"Sorry, hon."

I spoke into the tablet again. "Attention passenger and cargo. We will be enduring a short period of weightlessness, so be prepared. Captain Knolls out."

"I don't think I've ever been weightless before," Destiny said.

"We were weightless for a couple of minutes when the tube docked with the ship," I said.

"Yeah, but I was strapped in. What's it like?"

I grinned. "Get a barf bag, it upsets some folks' stomachs. I have to go to the pilot room, I'll be back shortly." I kissed her, threw the beer can at the noisy maid and walked to the pilot room.

Chapter Twelve

Weightless

It would be a couple of minutes before we were completely weightless. I lowered the throttle to zero G and swung the boat around. Gravity slowly went away as I dropped the throttle and stuff started floating a little. When I'd turned it around and given it enough power to slow us to to the right speed so Bill could catch us, the floating stuff slowly started dropping, and when the gauges said we were at the right speed I shut the throttle all the way down. Stuff started floating around again.

Shit, I forgot about the coffee. I flew back to my cabin – and I mean I literally flew through the air like a bat out of hell, since there was no gravity.

Destiny was floating above the couch. I pushed against the doorway towards the coffee table, hooked the pot down, and floated over to her after a gentle push against the wall. "I like this," she said. "Lets make love, I've never been weightless before."

"Well, I have, but I never made love when I was weightless before," I said.

Having sex without any gravity wasn't easy. Gravity makes almost everything easier.

An hour and a half later my fone buzzed. "John? Bill here, I'm almost at you, can you adjust speed and trajectory and dock the boats?"

"Yeah, I'll be in the pilot room in a second." I set my fone to the shipwide speakers. "Attention, passenger and cargo. We will be experiencing low gravity for a while followed by more zero gravity, so if you've been floating around with nothing to grab, now's your chance. You might want to strap down."

After some simple maneuvers, they're in the logs, I docked with Bill's ship and started both of our boats moving faster. Of course, once we undocked and I went back to regular speed I'd have to check the engines again. He called. "John, you want me to come over?"

"You bet, old buddy. I ain't seen you in ages!"

"See you in a minute."

"I'm going to cargo," I said to Destiny. "Want to come along?"

"And miss meeting one of your friends? Try to stop me!"

God, but I'd fallen in love with this woman. If it hadn't been for her the whores would have had me by now. There were probably seventy or eighty of them, naked of course, in the commons area, I noticed as we walked past in the low gravity.

We met Bill at the dock, one floor down over the generator; it was next to machine storage and about two stories high. There was a six by six meter airlock in the middle of the docking bay door and a rail where you had a four story high view of the generator.

The door opened and Bill came in. "Bill, meet Destiny," I said. "She's an astronomer and, uh, I guess my best friend."

Bill said "I thought I was your..." and looked at Destiny. "Oh. Damn but I'm dumb. Pleased to meet you, Destiny. You hooked up with this guy? And I thought scientists were supposed to be smart!"

I laughed. "Fuck you, Bill. Want a beer?"

"You have beer? I was wondering what you were hauling. I thought you didn't do cargo runs any more?"

"Well, this one's different. It ain't your normal cargo."

"If beer ain't your cargo why do you have beer?"

"I like beer! My houseboat's half full of it. I have wine,

too."

"Hell... can you spare some, old buddy?"

"Sure, I brought plenty. I can spare a few bottles of wine, too."

"Wow, thanks!" he said. "No wonder I like you so much, you old asshole!" We both laughed. "So," he said, "what's your cargo and why are you so rich right now?"

"Whores."

"Huh?"

"I'm hauling whores. They gave me a fifty percent bump in pay to haul 'em."

"Christ, you always get the good assignments! How the hell did you manage this one?"

"Hell if I know, the fucking CEO himself called me into his office. Scared the shit outta me."

"You must be livin' right!"

I laughed. "Me? Damn, Bill, you know me better than that. The extra money don't come anywhere near making up for the pain in the ass them women is, though."

Bill said "Uh, 'scuse me, Miss, uh..."

"Name's Destiny, Bill," she said.

"Uh, can I have a word in private with John?"

She looked at me and winked. "Sure, Bill." She took off, knowing full well I'd tell her what happened later, or maybe just reading Bill's mind, which wasn't very hard to do right then.

"Okay," Bill said, "Uh, look, John, uh, I ain't been laid in like forever and you got hookers on board your ship. Uh, you mind if I spend a little money while I'm on your boat?"

"Bill, I am about to make your day," I said. "No, I'm gonna make your *year!* You're gonna get laid and it ain't gonna cost you a penny. These bitches are horny as hell. They're so horny they'd pay you for it if they had any money. If you want an orgy, just go to my commons area, there's a hell of a lot of naked, horny whores waiting for you there. Meanwhile, I'll gradually accelerate a little more for a while while those batteries are being charged back up, no sense in both of us being late."

"Damn, buddy," Bill said. "You're the best friend I ever had!"

I winked at him. "All for the company's bottom line. Make sure that's in your logs!"

"Christ, John, of course!"

"Look, Bill, have fun with the whores and I'll meet you in my quarters after you get your rocks off."

Bill owes me! ...and, well, I guess I owe him, too. Maybe the whores will leave me alone for a while, I had Destiny. I didn't need no fucking whores, they were just a damned pain in my ass. I want a raise! Fifty percent more ain't enough to put up with them damned bitches.

It would have been a lot different without Destiny. The whores would have probably took over my boat by now.

I went back to the pilot room and sent paper to the company about the batteries, wondering why I had to send paper for a battery jump. I mean shit, I only charged them with my generator. It ain't like it cost anybody any money. Damned bureaucrats.

Then I recalculated trajectory... well, at least that's what the computer said it was doing, I get confused by those big words. I think "recalculate" means "do arithmetic" and "trajectory" means whatever map we're following but I ain't too awful sure. Anyway, then I raised gravity up a little more, but only to point two six since Bill's boat was docked to mine and I didn't want to damage the docking ring. We were moving faster now.

When I got back to my quarters, Destiny said "You should talk to Tammy."

"Huh? Why?"

"She's not a simple street hooker, she holds two PhDs, one in anthropology and one in psychology. She was studying the droppers when she got hooked."

"How the hell could that happen?"

"I don't know, ask her. "

"I can't, I was kind of an asshole when I first met her. I had to of course, but that doesn't make me feel any better about it."

"She likes you, John. She said that's one of the reasons."

"Huh? She likes me because I was an asshole?"

"She likes you because you aren't one of the stupid knuckle draggers that would have let her on board for a blow job. She said it showed you had good character, and I told her I wouldn't have been with you if you hadn't.

"She's really nice, really. I like her. Lets have coffee with her tomorrow."

"Uh, okay, I guess."

The doorbell buzzed. "Who is it?" Destiny said.

"Wild Bill Corpse. Jesus... them whores damned near killed me! But what a way to die!" he said as the door opened. He was smiling wider than I'd ever seen anybody smile.

"Did the robots finish charging the batteries?" he asked.

"No," I said. "It will be another hour. Is anybody but me hungry?"

Bill grinned even wider. "I just ate! Damn, John, thanks! Hey, can I take a few with me?"

"Get paper from the company and I'll do anything you want. But not without it, you know that."

He laughed. "You thought I was serious? Damn, John, I'd never do anything to get you in trouble. Especially after tonight. God! This might be the highlight of my whole damned life!"

"It'll be an hour before the batteries are finished charging," I said. "Lets eat something, I'm hungry. Come on, Bill, pussy isn't very filling. How about pizza?"

"I could go for pizza," Destiny said. "Bill?"

"Sure. Got a beer to go along with it?"

"Yeah, my houseboat's half full of beer, didn't I tell you? Have a beer and take a few cases with you. Robot, take six

53

cases of beer and six bottles of wine from my houseboat and transfer them to Captain Kelly's ship."

"Damn, John..."

"Look, Bill, what you did for me after that Jupiter run... you know. I couldn't have a better friend. You could have been ruined but you stuck up for me anyway. Ain't many people I know would do that." I chuckled. "My Mom, um, probably wouldn't."

"Well, John," Bill said, "What about high school? You stood up to bullies for me, and more than once, too. How was that any different?"

A table with a sliced pizza and three beers and three plates and some napkins on top of it rolled over to us. Destiny put on some twentieth century classical guitar, I don't remember who but she played all the old greats. We both love the music from that era.

We talked and laughed and ate pizza and drank beer and had a really good time and promised each other to keep in touch.

Bill shook my hand again and went back to his boat, and I lowered gravity to zero while the docking retractors retracted the docking mechanism. Or something, I ain't went to college.

I raised gravity to point two for twenty minutes to let him speed up first, so he would be ahead if he had more trouble. If he was going to have more problems it would be when the engines weren't all the way heated up. Running on batteries... shit. But I'd still have to pass him to get to Mars on time.

Of course, after turning the boat around I had to inspect the generators and engines. A robot was working on number forty two, so I logged it. Everything else was normal so I went back to my quarters.

Destiny and me didn't bother with a movie, we just went straight to bed.

Chapter Thirteen

Addiction

I woke up before her for once. I took a shit... hey, you wanted everything, right? Started the coffee because the robots really suck at making coffee, took a shower, and got dressed. I was just taking my first sip when the doorbell rang. It was Tammy.

"Hi," she said, "Uh, Destiny invited me over for coffee."

"Yeah, she told me last night. Come on in. She's still asleep, I'll get you a cup."

"Thanks."

"Uh," I said, handing her a cup, "Destiny says you're a psychologist and a, uh, I forgot what. You're not a whore, you're studying them."

"Did destiny tell you that?"

"She didn't have to. I ain't went to college but I ain't stupid, I can add two and two and get something between three and five. I got it when she told me you had two doctorates. It was obvious then."

"Is was?"

"Yeah, I wondered how you got the money for a ticket, but shit, you got two doctorates. You ain't gotta look for work. And I bet you ain't a dropper, neither. You're wearing clothes."

"No, I'm not a dropper and yes, I'm studying them. Want to know about my studies?"

"Huh? Why would I want to know that much about a bunch of damned whores?"

"Jesus, but you're a dumbass, John. I'm studying drug addiction and prostitution and you have two hundred drug addicted prostitutes on board and you don't have a clue how dangerous they are! Do you want an education, dumbass?"

I felt like a dumbass. "Dangerous? Yeah, I guess it might help." They never mentioned dangerous when they gave me this damned assignment.

"Here," she said, giving me a small memory chip.

"What's this?"

"Just read it. Don't worry, I can explain anything you don't understand."

Shit, I hate reading. That's one thing that me and Destiny are different about, she loves reading. "Well, you had me fooled when I met you," I said.

She laughed. "I study them, you don't know anything about them at all. Don't let them know they're being studied or the study will be ruined."

"I'm discreet. I Guess I have some studying to do."

"It'll save you a whole lot of trouble and just might save your life, and believe me, John, your life is in serious danger. I have some studying to do myself," Tammy said. "Tell Destiny to drop by when she wakes up, I'll be in the commons." She left, with her cup of coffee the robots didn't make. Nobody likes that nasty robot coffee.

It was almost eight and Destiny was still asleep. Oh, well. I went to the pilot room like normal, and decided to put inspection off a while, they're not "time-critical" (that's corporate bureaucrat talk) like the eight o'clock readings and adjustments are.

Everything checked out in the pilot room, so I went back to my living room and put the chip in the tablet and started reading. Destiny was still asleep. She was awake about ten minutes later and I drank coffee with her while the robots cooked scrambled eggs and bacon, and we had breakfast before I started reading again. She had her nose in a tablet, too.

After reading for an hour and a half I had to put the tablet down; I was in deep trouble. No wonder they was paying me so good.

Most of these girls were abused and sexually molested as children, and most of them were raised in foster care. Many and maybe most were children of criminal parents; alcoholics, drug abusers, gangsters, thieves, often very violent thieves. They were the kids that society allowed to be ruined for life.

It was sad. Most of them were droppers. There's a chemical name for drops in Tammy's book but I'd have to look it up and I can't pronounce it anyways.

These girls hated sex, their ever having a normal sex life was ruined in their childhoods when they were molested and abused. But drops made the whores enjoy getting fucked. Most of them had never had an enjoyable sexual experience until they put a drop in an eye before work.

There were other psycho-affective effects, and yeah, I had to look that and lots of other shit up when I read that damned book. Her book had a lot of other big words like neu-rotransmitters and chemical names and names of hormones and stuff and I just kind of glossed over them, I ain't never went to college or nothing.

There was a video of a dropper getting high. At least it was a break in reading. She sat in a chair leaning back, dropped a drop in each eye and dropped the dropper and kind of went limp for a minute. Then groaned, and a few seconds later started rubbing her breasts and crotch. Then she took off her pants and masturbated with a big dildo for a few minutes, had a very loud orgasm, sat there hugging herself for a few more minutes, then picked up the dropper and did it again.

I gathered the whores just stayed really fucked up all the time.

And the drug was highly addictive physically as well as being dangerous in worse ways. It made the user the opposite of pissed off when under the influence. When that was taken away, well... it ain't pretty.

"Damn," I thought, "Addiction must be a bitch" as I got another cup of coffee.

It seemed I was in for serious trouble. I needed to finish reading that book, but I still had inspections. I'd just inspected the engines and generators last night after Bill had left so it was probably going to be an easy day today.

It was. A different kind of robot was working on engine number forty two than last night so I logged it. I wondered what was wrong with it but hell, I have no idea how those things work. I just follow the checklist like they trained me.

Destiny was eating lunch when I got home. It was late and I was hungry again so I had the robot make me a turkey sandwich. She put on some silly old science fiction movie about time travel. Silly, but enjoyable. We ate cheeseburgers and coleslaw and potato salad for dinner and watched an old two dimensional movie about werewolves that didn't have any colors.

Huh? It was a horror movie, not the least bit believable but still entertaining. It was about a guy who gets bitten by a wolf and turns into one whenever there's a full moon and goes around killing some people and turning others into werewolves. Destiny said they were also called some weird long word I don't remember, I think it starts with an L. Then we watched another old gray horror movie called "Dracula".

We went to bed early after watching it.

Chapter Fourteen

Meteors

The damned alarm woke me up. Damn them whores... always causing trouble when I'm in the middle of something, like a good night's sleep. At least I'd gone to bed early last night, it was six in the damned morning.

But it wasn't the whores, it was a meteor shower. Fuck. I went to the pilot room.

The meteors were tiny but when you're going fast, well, when a meteor shower is coming you want to slow down.

Or speed up. Usually it was slow down but not this time. I spoke into the fone. "Attention, passenger and cargo. Prepare for higher gravity in ten seconds." Ten seconds later I gradually added thrust. We were almost at Earth-normal now, and man it was not the least bit comfortable. I felt like I weighed a ton.

After these long interplanetary trips it was usual to spend a week or two in a gradually faster centrifuge at one point three normal if you were landing on Earth, because after a few weeks of a third or less to three quarters gravity, Earth gravity was heavy as hell. While traveling, the gravity slowly changed from close to the body you left to a little more than the body you were landing on, whether a planet, a dwarf, or a satellite.

Except Earth, nobody was at a gravity higher than Earth. Of course, there are some planets heavier but you can't land on them or you'd get squished. Venus would feel like Earth but you can't land on Venus because it's just too damned hot, so the heaviest you were going to be was Earth. Even

Ganymede was a lightweight, lots smaller than Mars and it's the biggest satellite in the solar system.

After a few days of the centrifuge after you reached Earth, Earth gravity felt pretty good. I think I saw something on the news about scientists researching ways to actually land people on Venus and maybe some day even terraform it like they were doing on Mars, but they can't even keep a robot alive for more than a few days there now.

Right now the gravity wasn't too comfortable, but we had to outrun those rocks. We'd be at point nine five seven gravities for the next hour, so it looked like I was going to be staying up this morning. I was glad I'd done the inspection late in the afternoon the day before or I'd worry about the engines and generators. It looked like today was going to be a really long day, anyway. I was glad we'd gone to bed early instead of drinking, this would have been hell with a hangover. I went to my quarters and made coffee, wishing again that robots could make decent coffee. Damned stupid robots.

I had the robots make scrambled eggs and bacon and flipped on the video in the dining room and saw the last quarter of the zero gravity football semifinals. That's one hell of a sport, too bad Memphis lost. Cleveland did play better, though, so they earned the win.

I was wishing we were back to half gravity again, just sitting here was tiring. When the game was over I headed back to the pilot room.

I couldn't get in; there were over fifty whores blocking the hallway, all of them stoned on those God damned drops. "You're all going to be confined to quarters for the rest of the trip if you don't let me through," I said. "What you're doing is mutiny, you might even wind up in prison when we reach Mars." I wondered why they were up this early, but I *had* made an announcement that we were going to get heavy. I wished I hadn't.

One of them laughed. "You and whose army? You think you can take us all on?"

I pulled out my taser. Most of them laughed. "Go inspect your boat, Joe." I don't know why the whores call me that, they know my name. The woman continued. "This full gravity is great, Joe, and we ain't givin' it up!"

"Look," I said, "this acceleration is going to need a course correction. I have to get in that pilot room!"

"Fuck off, Joe." Scattered giggling from the whores, like I said all stoned on those God damned drops. Whoever invented that shit needs a good old fashioned ass kicking. I put the taser away and turned around and slunk off to the cargo area. I sure wasn't looking forward to this.

Damn but the cargo area for machinery and storage was a lot longer off than at half G. I finally got there, suited up, and went through the airlock, because it was only other way into the pilot room besides the door the mutinous whores were blocking.

My God but I was scared. With the boat's acceleration it was like hanging from the side of a skyscraper. With weights on you. In a space suit with clumsy gloves.

I hooked the A tether to the highest rung I could reach and climbed. When the tether was below me I hooked the B tether above and unhooked the A tether.

I don't know how long it took me to get to the houseboat but it took a long damned time. I was sure glad the airlocks were upstairs, climbing maybe two stories was bad enough. I had to stop and rest a few times. I was sweating so hard I was afraid I'd drown in my own damned space suit.

I finally got there, did the airlock thing and went inside. They need to find a way to keep helmets from frosting up as soon as you leave the airlock, you can't see shit until you get your helmet off.

I took off the suit and went through the dock into the pilot room, pulling the suit in behind me. I was soaked in sweat, and I wouldn't have been wetter if I'd been caught in a thunderstorm on Earth.

All of my muscles ached, on fire. Them whores was going to be floating in a minute, I was really pissed off at them God damned bitches. I strapped into the pilot chair and killed the ion thrusters. The asteroid threat had long since passed and we'd been at high G way too long. Damn, we were way off course.

Well, I'd fix that later. Right now I had a bunch of whores to lock up, and I wasn't about to be gentle. I was hurting like hell from the climb, I stunk, I was really pissed off at them God damned whores and almost hoped they'd give me an excuse to tase them.

I was also looking forward to a shower. I was nasty; I'd had to go straight to the pilot room from bed and hadn't had my morning bath yet. And I'd had to climb up a God damned skyscraper at almost Earth gravity after being at only a little more than half for quite some time.

I checked the monitor – they were all still outside the pilot room, floating, trying to guard it from me, ignorant of how the houseboat was docked to the ship. I wonder what went through their heads when they started floating?

I pulled out my tasers and went outside. "All of you worthless God damned fucking bitches, hands behind your backs or God damn it I'm going to tase the shit out of you! NOW God damn it!"

This time they complied. It took half an hour to get them all cuffed and another half hour to get them to their rooms. I was going to miss the eight o'clock readings if I didn't hurry. I stopped by my quarters for a second to make sure Destiny was okay and get coffee if there was any made or start a pot if it wasn't, it was quarter to eight.

She wasn't there. I called on the fone but she wasn't answering. I knocked on Tammy's door. She opened it and said "You're probably looking for Destiny."

"Yeah, you seen her?"

"She was worried about you. She was heading toward the cargo bay right before we lost gravity."

Holy hell, I hoped she hadn't tried to go outside the

boat to find me, but she couldn't get into the cargo bay with the airlock, anyway; it was locked. If she had been able to, she would have probably been dead, or would be soon; that other suit hadn't had its air pack all the way filled and she'd have been out there almost an hour.

I kicked off as hard as I could towards the cargo hold, flying as fast as I could, glad that damned door was locked.

I tried calling her again but she still wasn't answering her fone.

The cargo hold door was open. That wasn't right, that door should always be closed. I had no idea how it got opened, they close and lock automatically when you let them close and nobody but me should have been able to get in. Whoever did get in must have propped it open. Did one of them whores hack the lock and throw Destiny over the railing? I went in, scared to death about her, looking over the rail for the bloody mess I was afraid I'd see. Nobody had been thrown over the rail, so I went in the next room, the one with an airlock and a docking bay.

The outside hatch of the airlock was open, which meant somebody was outside the boat. That relieved me a little, after I'd looked over the railing and not seen a bloody mess I'd worried that one of the whores had thrown her out of the airlock without a suit. But the open hatch said that thankfully hadn't happened.

It also said that I wasn't getting outside here. Thankfully there were three airlocks that doubled as boat docks. One was for the captain's houseboat connected to the pilot's room, and the other two were at opposite ends of the ship. Sometimes dozens of ships coupled like this traveled together. It's supposed to be cheaper that way for big loads.

I flew as fast as I could back to the pilot room, which was closer to both airlocks than either was to each other. I put on the suit again and went through the houseboat's airlock, closing it behind me. My suit was surely low on air, too, but I didn't worry about my air, I was too worried about Destiny's air.

The climb on the skyscraper-like boat was a lot easier without gravity. It was probably stupid of me and was way against company safety regulations, but I was in a hurry to get to Destiny, who was probably dying by now so I didn't bother with tethers, I just moved as fast as I could. She'd been out there a long time. My God but this woman was my life! The thought of losing her... I climbed faster.

Well, this time it wasn't like a climb; there wasn't anything pulling me down, there had been gravity the last time I was outside the boat. Right now there wasn't no such thing as down, although everywhere was down. It was more like running along the rungs with my hands and every step made me go faster. It's hard to explain.

I kept trying to call her on the suit radio, knowing it was useless. Her radio probably wasn't even turned on or she would have tried to call me rather than following me out.

After climbing for maybe ten or fifteen minutes I finally made it around to the airlock she'd left open and saw her floating about six or so meters from the boat. I hooked two tethers to a rung next to the airlock and one of them to my suit and pushed off towards her. She wasn't moving, and that worried the hell out of me. If she was conscious she'd be thrashing around in a panic. She was obviously out of air and maybe dead. Oh, God! Please don't let her be dead! I'm not religious but I prayed anyway. Jesus but I was terrified for her.

A suit alarm went off; my own oxygen was getting low; I'd been outside a long time on the first climb and hadn't filled my air or changed the filters. I hooked the second tether to her suit and climbed back to the boat on my own tether.

You would think climbing a tether without gravity pulling at you would be easy. You'd be wrong.

There's no gravity but there's still mass and the suit's gloves were bulky and clumsy. There was the mass of two humans and two suits, which weren't all that light. I climbed the tether to the lock and pulled her in behind me as the suit alarm went off again, this one saying I had too much carbon dioxide.

Finally we were inside the airlock, and of course as soon as the inside door opened I couldn't see because of the hoar frost that instantly condensed on the suit and helmet. Damned hoar! I shed my helmet and gloves and her helmet. She took a big gasp of air – she was alive! I got our suits off and a medic came in and took her away with an oxygen mask on her face.

Huh? Jesus, guys, they get around in zero gravity with compressed air. Why did they send you two guys? Jesus. They send two guys that ain't never been on a boat. What the hell?

I had a headache. That's what happens when you have too much carbon dioxide and not enough oxygen, and it makes it hard to think straight, too.

I floated back to the pilot room to make the course correction. It looked like the ship's inspection would be a little late today, but that's not "time critical" like the bureaucrats say. I thought it would be all right since I'd inspected twice the day before.

I was already really late for the eight o'clock adjustments, but it didn't matter today because I was going to have to make a course correction anyway. A big course correction.

I should have inspected the ship first.

Chapter Fifteen

Fusion

As I was floating back to the pilot room, Tammy was waiting outside her quarters, hanging from the doorway with one hand. "Is Destiny OK?" she asked with a worried tone.

"She will be," I said. "A little anoxia." They'd warned us about anoxia in captain's training, and I'd seen it before. Hell, I've experienced it myself before, it's sure not fun. "She's in the sick bay getting oxygen. You can see her if you want but she was still unconscious when the robot took her."

"Thanks. I would have thought you'd have stayed with her."

"God knows I would have liked nothing better, but I have to make sure we all get to Mars alive. We're off course and I have to inspect the ship to make sure it isn't about to blow up or anything. Look, I gotta go," I said as I continued to the pilot room.

We were even farther off course than I'd feared. Now it was a matter of juggling speed and fuel usage to the company's specifications. Fuel usage? I do *not* understand company policy, fuel for the generators is dirt cheap since they switched from fission generators to the fusions. Compared to the other costs it was free. It made sense back when they used fission generators but it makes no sense at all these days. But I'm just a ship's captain, what the hell do I know? It ain't like I ever went to college.

Back in the old days, a little before my time as a captain, these boats had fission generators and fuel really did matter on them. They also weren't so automated until they were retrofitted a few years before I took my training, that was about twenty years or so ago. I've been on the job since I graduated high school, more than a couple of decades ago. Before I started, back when they only had fission power, crews were human rather than robot and the captain had to calculate all this stuff by hand, with their primitive computers helping. Of course, the newer stuff was all phased in a ship at a time, so nobody had to get laid off. Normal turnover took care of that; the other transport companies pay better than ours even though their ships are cheap dangerous crap, and we were the first to automate. I was one of the first cheap uneducated captains on an automated ship, seven or eight years after the first one. I think when I was hired there were only a half dozen or so running the automated boats.

Captains had to go to college back before automation, and some of the crew, too. Since the captain had to figure out all that shit almost by hand he needed to know calculus. Hell, I ain't even took algebra even though I could have in high school.

I made the adjustments the computer read out, and we had gravity again and were going the right way. I didn't look at what gravity was, and how much gravity it was was hard to tell without looking at the gauges, since we'd been so heavy before weightlessness and we were weightless for a long time.

The empty passengers' quarters were first, then cargo pens. I wondered why they call them that. Shouldn't it be cargo quarters? As usual, the passenger section was fine.

Cargo is almost always a pain in the ass. "Who is it?" a voice said at my ring of the doorbell. Presumably Kathy, which was the name on the doorplate.

"Captain Knolls. Ship inspection, you girls should be used to this by now."

"Yeah, Joe? You should be used to us telling you to fuck off by now, too."

"Door, open. I can lock you up any time I want, you know. I don't even need no excuse to lock up cargo."

"I ain't got no drops, bitch."

I suddenly realized why they called them "pens". They were designed to house any species of animal, and a word Destiny had teased me for using came to mind.

Feral. From what I'd read of Tammy's book, some of these whores were more animal than human, especially when they didn't get their drops. It had driven Billie crazy enough that she'd wound up blowing her quarters up, with her in them. Apparently, withdrawal not only tortures the addict's mind, it introduces extreme pain in the muscles and joints. Withdrawal from the drops can be fatal, for innocent bystanders as well as the addict herself. Few droppers survived withdrawal. I should finish reading it, I guessed.

I sighed. "I hope you're lying. From what I found out I'm better off when you have them."

"Well, cough 'em up, Joe!"

I laughed, and replied "I ain't got no drops, bitch!"

I did wonder why they hadn't run out. Where were they getting them from? They shouldn't have been able to get them onto the boat in the first place.

Billie's quarters were next. She, along with some fifty odd fellow cargo, were confined for the duration because of the gravity mutiny. Of course, I just opened the door and entered, taser in hand. This would have been a "brig" back when Captains had to go to college and made a hell of a lot more money than I do.

The robots had done a good job, but they always did. Except for making coffee, they suck at that. And barbecue, but I don't think anybody eats barbecue in space. And they weren't any good that run I got stranded on. And they can't tell where an atmosphere leak is. I wonder why they're not programmed for that? But they did most things real good, you really couldn't tell that Billie had almost burned to death at all. Well, except that her hair was really short and frizzly.

"Inspection."

"I ain't got no drops, bitch."

"Whatever," I sighed, and inspected the quarters. It was obvious she was lying, her eyes gave her away. Droppers' eyes looked really weird when they were high. Usually the pupils were each different sizes. When they were going through withdrawal they were hellishly scary, like a wild animal's eyes. Going through withdrawal their pupils were so big there was almost no iris, and they were so bloodshot the whites looked red. I'd only seen a photo of one in Tammy's book and hoped I would never see it on the boat.

I wondered again where the drops were coming from.

After hearing "I ain't got no drops, bitch" so many times I didn't even hear it any more. I went to inspect the sick bay, the one part of the inspection I looked forward to. I wanted to see how Destiny was doing.

Tammy was sitting there talking with her. "John!" Destiny said. "Tammy told me you saved my life."

I blushed, and grinned sheepishly. "It's my job."

Tammy laughed. "Bullshit, any other 'cargo' wouldn't have made it. Destiny almost died, and she would have if you weren't moving so frantically. God but you're fast!"

Destiny pulled me close and kissed me. "Thanks, Johnnie," she whispered, "Tammy said you risked your life, that you had to have been going against the company's safety regulations or there would have been no way you would have gotten to me in time." Then she said in a normal voice "go ahead and finish your inspection, sweetheart, the gurney said I should be able to go home in half an hour or so. I'll meet you there."

There was a stairwell to get to the generators and engines, which were on the "bottom" of the boat, five stories down. Those engines are really huge. Damned cheap bastards should put a lift in.

The ion engines were in the "bottom" because the engines pushing against the ship pushed everything else the other way. Something about "three laws of thermoses" or something but I think I was hung over that morning's training and don't really remember. Something about actions and opposite reactions or something.

I went over the checklist and checked out the first engine. There were a awful lot of lot of the monstrously huge things. A hell of a lot of electricity goes through each one of them, too. It took almost two big fusion generators to fire them all up at maximum thrust. That's an ungodly amount of power.

I had two more engines to go when an alarm went off. "Damned whores, not now!" I thought.

But it wasn't the whores, it was the port generator and I couldn't get in; the computer said it was an inferno in there. Hell, that damned thing should have shut down automatically and all the air released. I pulled the circuit breaker and the shutdown switch and there was a sort of thump. Damn. Another trip to the pilot room, we were going to be off course again, at least a little. Plus I could hear wind, that would be the air evacuating. Air dumped fast like that from a room that big can set you a little off course, too.

It would have to cool before the robots could start repairing it, if it was repairable at all. Damn, if the other generator went out, too... at any rate I wouldn't be burning all the engines at full power, not that I'd ever had to before. You can get a gravity and a half at full power, they say. Right now we'd be lucky to get one gravity.

I called Destiny. "Honey, I'm really sorry but this is going to take a while."

Chapter Sixteen

Generator

I started the long walk back to the pilot room after trudging up the five God damned flights of stairs, wishing again for a bicycle or something. Hell, a lift would be even better. I was worn out from climbing and walking. And really hungry, it was past lunch time and I'd had breakfast really early and hadn't eaten anything since.

A robot wheeled past. Hell, I should just flag down one of the robots. But, of course there was a reason for not having transportation; I remembered the climb up the boat earlier in the morning when the mutinous whores kept me out of the pilot room and how tiring it was. My muscles were still on fire and I'd be worse the next day. A body needs exercise and the most I was going to get on a boat with two thirds gravity or usually not anywhere close to that was walking and climbing stairs.

Destiny and Tammy were in the commons with a few other women; I say "women" because these were acting halfway civilized, despite their lack of clothing, but they certainly wasn't ladies.

"Done already?" Destiny asked.

"No," I sighed. "Trouble. One of the generators blew out and we're off course again. I just saw you and thought I'd say 'hi', I can't stay. Too much damned work."

"What do you have to do? How long will it take?"

"I don't know. When I get us back on course I have to see what the robots are doing with that damned generator and if they can fix it."

"How bad is it?" Tammy asked. "How many generators are there?"

"Only two. I wish this was an old tub, they originally had just one fission generator and got retrofitted with fusions in addition later, when the cost of building fusion generators had dropped enough to be affordable. If our other generator dies it's batteries.

"What then?"

"Then we're late, and Mars will be more dangerous because of the damned pirates. But there isn't much chance of losing both generators, we'll be okay. But speaking of generators, I gotta go." I kissed Destiny and headed to the pilot room. It was only a minor correction, it's in the log. Then I went to check out the generator back down all those damned stairs, wishing I had time to eat.

It had cooled enough for the robots to go in to work, but was a bulkhead removed from where a human could stand it. I had two more engines I hadn't checked off as well, so I inspected them, too. Of course, if there was anything wrong I'd have been clueless. But all the readouts were what the tablet said they should be.

The repair robots said the generator was shot. Well, not exactly like that, of course. The readout just listed stuff, but basically what it listed was melted parts that we don't carry replacements on-board for, and parts that the whole damned thing has to be rebuilt to replace, like those lasers that are inside them. They have to completely rebuild the generator if the lasers went kerflooey, anyway, and I'm pretty sure the robots couldn't do that even if they had the parts. Wild Bill could have probably hacked something together to make it work, he's pretty much a nerd... but then, he couldn't get his own generators working and was now riding on batteries he had to charge from my generators. Of course, there had been paperwork to charge his boat's batteries. Damned bureaucrats.

Shit.

After climbing all those damned stairs again I walked

past the commons to my quarters. Destiny and Tammy weren't in there although there were a few unclothed whores. Damn it, women, at least put some underwear on!

Destiny and Tammy were in my living room drinking coffee. As I walked in, Destiny said "John, you're damned lucky Tammy's here."

As I'd suspected. "You're supplying the drops," I said, sitting down.

"Yeah."

"The whores would have killed us without them."

"Yeah."

"How much you got?"

"Plenty."

"Enough to get us all to Mars alive?"

"Don't worry. I know my chemistry and psychology and physiology, I know how much they need."

I said "Don't give any to the bitches in confinement."

"You never finished that book, did you? You don't know what you're talking about. With drops they're harmless. Take them away, and well, it isn't pretty."

I was confused. "What can they do locked up?"

"They might rip the doors off and kill us all, or if they can't they're liable to suicide. A mindless withdrawing dropper can die even in a straitjacket. Most droppers are dead before they're thirty. Finish reading that book!"

Crap. Losing cargo is a pretty bad thing. Especially since they were human beings this time, instead of cattle or something.

I always hated shipping cows. They stink. Hogs are even worse, but it isn't often anybody ships pigs anywhere. Nobody can afford pork, thank God.

"I will. Crap! Damn but I'm glad you're here. I'm going to suggest to the company that they send someone like you on all these runs."

She laughed. "The company wouldn't want to spend the money necessary. The bean counters know how much loss is

73

acceptable."

Destiny said "I made coffee."

"Thanks," I said, "but after the day I've had I want a beer and some lunch."

"I'm still trying to wake up," she said.

"Yeah, you napped for an hour or so after you went for a stroll outside. I would have thought the oxygen would have made you wake up. Computer, sausage pizza and a beer."

"Actually, the oxygen put me to sleep," she said.

I had to ask. "Why in the hell did you pull that stunt, sweetheart? My God, I almost lost you!"

She turned as red as a beet. "I don't know, John, I just panicked. I thought you were going to die out there."

"Why didn't you call?"

"I don't know. Because I'm an idiot, I guess. I just didn't think of it. God, John, I'm really sorry."

"Well..." I said.

Pizza takes a while to cook, but where in the hell was that robot with my beer? "Robot! Beer, damn it, are you deaf?" A robot rolled over with my beer. I'm glad this boat has the older robots, because the newer ones talk, and it's annoying as hell. If I want output from the computer I'll use my fone or a tablet and just read what it has to say.

Tammy said she had drug addicts to study and excused herself. I figured she had whores to supply drops to. I was starved, I hadn't had time to shower and hadn't had anything to eat since breakfast. I finished my beer and took a shower while the robots made lunch... What? Prime rib, baked potato and salad with a glass of wine; you know, poor people food.

The damned robot must not have heard me asking for pizza earlier, those things should beep or something. Anyway, lunch was done cooking when I got out of the shower and I had the robot open a bottle of wine. After lunch we watched some really dumb old movie from a couple hundred years ago, laughing all the way through it, although they say when it was made, it was meant to be serious.

Lunch had been really late, so dinner was late, too. We had turkey and dumplings, mashed potatoes and gravy, and green beans.

Then we cuddled a while to some old classical music, a band with Page and Clapton. It was early but we went to bed anyway, I was really beat. I hoped tomorrow would be less stressful. My muscles all ached from the walking and climbing, and I was going to be in hurting like hell the next day.

Chapter Seventeen

Alarms

All of my muscles were on fire when I woke up. We would have had to turn the ship around today, and in fact that's what was scheduled, except for the meteors and the drama that followed added a week to the time to turn around. Damned whores!

Destiny was sleeping peacefully. I got up, thankful that we weren't at Earth gravity but wishing we had turned around for deceleration then, because they have it plotted so that you start the journey close to the planet you're leaving's gravity, and reach your destination close to that planet's gravity; we'd started the trip at point seven five gravities. We were at half Earth gravity now and it would gradually be lowering to Mars' gravity as we got closer. If we were closer, gravity would be less and walking wouldn't hurt so much.

The droppers didn't like half Earth gravity, they were going to hate Mars. I guess these girls were being well paid or something, they sure were paying me good. Except that from what I'd learned about these women they probably just promised free drops. Drops were the addicts' only motivation, only goal, only thing that mattered to them. I needed to finish reading that damned book.

God but my muscles were all on fire, I was in real pain. I headed to the kitchen to make coffee but sat down on the couch on the way there and had the robot make a cup of shitty coffee; my legs hurt and I didn't feel like standing up yet. I had it bring me water and Naproxen and drank the lousy coffee. Yech. Nasty. Why can't they program those damned things to make drinkable coffee? I should have went to college and learned programming.

I only drank half of the nasty brew and hauled myself painfully to the shower after telling the robots to cook my breakfast. A hot shower would do wonders for my aching muscles.

The hot water felt as good as the coffee had tasted bad. I took a really long, extra hot shower. It helped ease the pain, and the pill I had taken started working some, too.

I took one sip of the remaining cold, nasty coffee and started a pot. Damned stupid robots.

I was just pouring a cup when Destiny came in the kitchen. "John!" she said. "You really look like hell!"

"I imagine I do. I sure feel like hell," I said, sitting down to eat my breakfast. Huh? Over easy, toast, steak, and hash browns. Anyway, I added "All that damned climbing in high gravity yesterday nearly killed me. And I still have to check the instruments and inspect the boat."

"You did inspections all day yesterday. Can't you take a sick day?"

"Nope, I just have to tough it out. And yesterday wasn't the least bit normal and I have tons of work to do today. I have to inspect that busted generator since it would have cooled enough by now, and the other one, too, since it's working harder now that there's only one. Besides, engine and generator inspections are every day."

"Poor baby!"

"Well, at least I don't have to inspect upstairs today. Want to watch a movie later?"

"Sure. Isn't it almost time to check your instrumentation?"

"Yeah, it is." I used a napkin and then kissed her. "See you in a while."

I filled my coffee and went towards the pilot room, which was really just outside my quarters. Yesterday I'd been wishing for a bicycle, today I was wishing for a pair of crutches, or at least a cane. My arms and legs ached and my back was killing me, I must have pulled it dragging Destiny back in the ship.

All the readouts were normal except one – air pressure in the port generator was twenty kilopascal low. That wasn't a good sign at all, I was going to need a suit and tether in case a bulkhead blew while I was in there. Damn. I did *not* want to wear a suit today! Or climb five flights of stairs both ways but I'd have to do that anyway, leak or no leak.

I noted the log and stopped by our cabin... heh, "our cabin," how about that? Anyway I stopped to fill a big mug with more coffee – real coffee, not that robot crap, and summoned a medic.

I laid down on the medic and ordered it to the port generator and got the computer on the fone and had it have a robot put air in the suit from the starboard hold where Destiny had gone out the airlock, change out the carbon dioxide scrubbers and bring it to me. I should have rode a robot yesterday, especially up that damned five flights of stairs from the engine deck.

I don't know how the robots go up and down stairs, because they move on wheels, but the medic kept me level and didn't even lurch. Maybe that's what that rail under the handrail is for.

After I'd suited up and tethered, the difference in pressure between the two rooms made it hard to get the hatch open. I tried a crowbar and couldn't even make it hiss. So I lowered the pressure where I was and the door popped open by itself. I took a floater with me to hunt for the leak.

What? You guys don't know what a floater is? What the hell, you guys work for a shipping and transportation company and never been in a boat? A floater is just a small balloon filled with helium with a little counterweight to make it gravity neutral. It follows the air and goes where the air goes. We get plenty of helium from the generators, the company should sell the stuff. Maybe they already do, I don't know.

I found where the air was escaping and patched it. Why can't they program robots to do that? Stupid robots, they could act as maids and cooks and medical doctors and mechanics and all sorts of other things but the damned stupid robots can't patch a hole or make a decent cup of coffee. At least they're cheap to manufacture. Maybe that's why, maybe programs are expensive. My robots sure were expensive, even though they were cheap to build.

The pressure was slowly rising, so I sat on the medic and waited until it matched the rest of the ship so I could get out of the room. Thankfully I hadn't needed the suit, but left it on just to keep my ears from popping.

The gauge said pressure was normal so I tried the hatch. It opened easy, so I took off the suit and gave it to a robot and continued the inspection. I was glad that except for the leak, the engines and generators gave me no problems. I rode the medic back to my rooms.

I was dying of thirst, even after downing that big glass of water when I took the naproxin. I said something to Destiny about it when I got back, taking another pill and drinking more water.

She laughed. "You're dehydrated, dummy. You told me yesterday you thought you were going to drown in your suit from sweating. You probably need electrolytes, too."

"And I'm hungry, I only ate part of my breakfast. Ran out of time," I said. "You hungry?"

"I didn't even eat breakfast today, I could eat. Robot eggs okay or do you want me to cook?"

"No, robots cook okay as long as it doesn't involve coffee or barbecue sauce. They never use enough salt but there's saltshakers. How do you want your eggs?"

"Ham and cheese omelette is okay, maybe with some hash browns," she said, grinning.

I laughed. "With caviar?"

She giggled. I said "Okay, funny girl, what do you really want?"

She laughed again. "Steak and cheese omelette, I guess. And hash browns."

"Okay," I said. "Robot, a steak and cheese omelet, a Denver chicken omelette, two hash browns and white toast. *No coffee!*"

Them damn robots suck at coffee, and they can't patch a hole at all. I'm glad they can cook. Well, except for barbecue, they suck at that, too. But who has barbecue in space?

We started a movie after brunch. The alarm went off when we were watching it; a real movie this time, a modern holo rather than the ancient two dimensional ones we'd been watching. I don't know what it was called, it was set in the eighteenth century and was about spies. So of course when the alarm went off I thought "damned whores." But it might not have been droppers, the computer was reporting another fire.

"Sorry, hon, we have a fire in the commons. I'll be back when I can."

When the red light is lit over most doors, they can only be opened from the inside unless you're the captain. When it flashes red outside it won't let you in, when it flashes red on the inside you'd better get the hell out of there *right now*.

There were a few exceptions, like my quarters. It would only keep me in if there was a vacuum or a fire outside the door. It only flashed yellow as a warning.

Another alarm went off when I was on my way to the commons. What the hell? This one was in the passenger section, apartment twelve. Nobody should be in there. Addicts? More electric problems?

The commons was closer and I had to make sure the cargo had evacuated, anyway.

There wasn't no whores in the commons, not even the blonde, and there wasn't no fire, either. The whores must have all been asleep; droppers sleep a lot and it was late afternoon, at least according to ship's clocks, which would reset themselves when we got to Mars.

My tablet reported it was a scheduled drill. That explained number twelve, sometimes they simulated more than one fire at a time. Stupid simulations.

It went off again. "Fire in cargo section, pen number six." I laughed, the computer was posing a conundrum for me. And for the cargo, too. If your quarters caught fire you were supposed to go to the commons, but what if the commons was on fire, too? Didn't they ever think of stuff like that?

Number six... that was one of the Thai girls, wasn't it?

There was screaming from the other side of the door. "Computer, open the door" I ordered.

"Unable to comply. Danger to ship, passenger, other cargo, and crew."

God DAMN that fucking computer. "Report."

"Fire in cargo hold six. Fire suppression technologies deployed."

The damned thing talks like it's went to college.

"Let those girls out, God damn it!!"

"Unable to com..."

"GOD DAMN IT!!"

And then another damned alarm went off. Son of a bitch! "Computer, source of new alarm."

"Meteor shower ahead." Holy shit but that was bad. Thankfully, the door opened right then and two of the three Thai girls stumbled out, along with the fat German, coughing. Smoke billowed from the door before it closed as a medic rolled up.

"Meet me in the commons, I have an emergency," I said. I ran to the pilot room on my sore legs, my back aching something terrible.

This time, like most times, meteors meant slow down and I was glad of it. I reduced gravity to ten percent, and my back didn't seem to hurt as much. This time I wasn't going to face the whores until it was over, we were already behind schedule and I was starting to see that they really hated low gravity a lot.

After the rocks all passed in front of us I sped back up

and adjusted course to make up for the damned rocks.

I checked the passenger quarters and sure enough it was a drill. What morons program this shit, anyway? Having emergency drills when there's a real emergency? And worse, two real emergencies! That's dangerous as all hell. Stupid dangerous. Those bozos might have went to college but they were stupid morons. God damned idiots, no common sense at all!

What? Yeah, yeah, just shut up and let me talk, I want to get this over with. Anyway, the three girls were still sitting on the medic outside the apartment sucking oxygen when I got back. The door light was red but no longer flashing.

"So what happened?" I asked them.

"Don't know," the obese German blonde wheezed in her heavily accented English. I can never remember her name, she's "the one with the German accent." Anyway, after coughing for a minute she says, with her heavy German accent of course, "we were just talking when that damned noisy maid burst into flames and the room locked us in! We were scared shitless!"

It happened sometimes, but they usually smoked for a while before they started burning, and then only when they were old and worn out. I hoped this ship had a robot that made robots, or at least a robot that could fix burned up robots. Sometimes some of these boats are missing some of their equipment.

The light went out, the door opened, the Thai women went in and the blonde went home. So did I.

Destiny had fallen asleep on the couch, so I had the robot make me a hamburger and get me a beer and I put the movie back to where it was when I left.

Chapter Eighteen

Pirates

Not much happened in the next few days that I didn't log in the ship's log, even though I've been talking about it all damned day long today. Is anybody really going to read this whole damned thing? You don't need to know every time I take a shit or what I had for breakfast, right? Even though I went into detail about those days. I bet nobody's going to read *that*. Anyway, the whores pretty much behaved themselves. It was like taking a vacation almost, except inspections and checking the systems in the morning. Even the cargo inspections didn't have anything happening, and the engines and the good generator were behaving themselves as well.

Like the log says, robots were trying to fix the busted generator but I knew they couldn't because they didn't have any parts, and it was going to have to be rebuilt even if the stupid robots did have parts and they're not programmed to rebuild generators, even if they were in a repair shop. They're programmed to try to do what they're programmed to do no matter how impossible doing it is. They'll spend days searching for parts that aren't listed in the computer's database when they should know better. I mean, can't the stupid robots access the databases? I don't know if programming them like that is smart or dumb, but idiots programmed them to make coffee, that's for sure. Maybe they weren't idiots, maybe they just didn't drink coffee and their bosses were idiots for assigning somebody who didn't drink coffee to program a robot to make coffee, I don't know.

Anyway, after an easy couple of days there were some

more little rocks in our way, but these were mapped; we could just go around them. The computers would do the actual steering but I have to sit in the pilot seat in case the four of them disagree about something and I have to make a decision. I've never seen them disagree about anything ever since I started driving these boats, though.

While we were driving around the rocks, Wild Bill called over the maser link. "John, Bill here. I'm about a light minute ahead of you and I'm standing still again, but this time it's on purpose. There's pirates ahead, and I can't outrun them on batteries. If your systems are all in good shape, run like hell. If you're having problems you should stop."

Shit. I could out run them on one generator easy but what if the other one went out? Hell, I could just detour around them. Too bad Bill didn't have that advantage, batteries just didn't hold enough energy. I have no idea how in the hell he was still in front of me on only batteries. Well, come to think of it we'd gone way off course when we were doing almost a full gravity, that's probably when he passed me. Orbital mechanics is weird, I have no idea how the computers figure that shit out. Bill was sure getting more speed out of batteries than I could, though. But Bill's a nerd, he likes reading tech manuals and boring stuff like that.

I answered him back. "Pirates? This far out? Are you sure they're pirates?" You usually only saw pirates near Mars. Ships full of cargo, all decelerating, make it easier for pirates to catch. You never saw pirates this far away from Mars. Shipping is usually pretty safe this far out.

It would be a couple of minutes before I heard back. I put the course correction into the computers' input console while I waited, then addressed the folks on board. "Passenger and cargo, your attention, please. Prepare for unexpected gravity changes. Strap down, ladies, it might be wild. That is all."

Bill answered. "It's a fleet and they're not listed in the computer. Hell if I know what they're doing way out here. I reported it to headquarters and they have a fleet on course to meet us, but we're still a long way off, way too far for them to do us any good now."

Damn. Bill was a damned good friend who had helped me out of jams more than once. And he was hauling tons of different metals, a valuable cargo inside a valuable ship. His short circuit could have been sabotage; pirates have been known to infiltrate the company before. This could be a trap for Bill and his ship and cargo.

The company wouldn't too much mind pirates killing Bill but they'd hate to lose the ship and cargo, so maybe I wouldn't get in *too* much trouble for what I planned, even though it was way outside the book and completely against company regulations. I picked up the fone and addressed the ship's P.A. System again. You can probably get a lot more detail from the computers, but anyway I got on the P.A. "Attention, ladies, this is the captain," I said. "When I said strap down, I meant it. Strap down, we're going to have some crazy gravity in a few minutes and if you're not strapped down it's really gonna hurt bad. That is all."

I strapped into the pilot's chair myself. I turned the boat around and decelerated, lowered power to half the engines, made one look like it was sputtering, and informed Bill to get ready. Then I went toward the pirates while the computers figured out the trajectory, or whatever the computers figure, for what I'd planned. I'm glad I have those computers, I could never do the math myself. Hell, I'd have to know calculus.

They saw me, and I pretended I'd just noticed them and changed course. I wasn't kidding when I told the women gravity was going to be weird. The maids were going to be busy, I'm sure.

They took chase. I went just slow enough to keep them the right distance and get where I was headed when I was headed there. Timing really mattered.

From the radar it looked like they were steering those

things by hand. Good, that raised my chances. Actually there wasn't any danger to me since I could outrun 'em easy and they can't shoot at me or do anything that might damage the boat and cargo, because their goal is to get the boat and cargo, both incredibly valuable. Our company brags that its ships "are almost impervious to weapons," anyway, even if other companies' aren't. But it raised my chances of saving Bill and his ship.

You know how the pirate fleets work, with a lead ship carrying an EMP. They don't know we designed these ships with pirates in mind and their EMP wouldn't stop us, but the EMPs will stop boats owned by other companies. And I didn't want them to know so I sent them a nice little present, fired from the rail gun.

I hear the pirates still use chemicals like gunpowder or something in their weapons. But hell, with all the tremendous amounts of energy coming out of those giant fusions, who needs chemicals?

The bastard's ship exploded and we were almost there...

When I reached the right spot I raised all the engines to full power, or as full as one generator would give me, and we took off like a bat out of hell. Ten seconds later the poor pirates got caught in the rain, as we say. I thought they probably all died. I sure hoped so, murderous bastards after my friend!

I set the course back to Mars and addressed the ladies. "You can unstrap now."

Time for another inspection, since I'd pushed her hard on one generator, and even turning them around breaks stuff sometimes. No, usually *something* breaks when you turn around, even if it's minor.

Like it says in the log, the generator was fine but a little warm. The engines were in good shape, too, but I shut down the one I made stutter for twenty four hours, just like the book says. For once nothing had broke.

This called for a beer. Hell, this called for champagne but I didn't have any, who can afford that anyway? Might as well be eating pork. I started back to my quarters for a beer.

Chapter Nineteen

โต้เถียงอย่างรุนแรง

I heard cats fighting again on my way home: the Thai girls. They always sounded like house cats fighting when they argued. I looked in the commons area and they were nose to nose and looked like they would be coming to blows pretty soon.

Damned whores. The pay raise wasn't enough for me to put up with this shit. First pirates way out here where you never saw pirates, and now the whores were acting up. "Knock it off, you two," I said. "Now, what's going on?" I demanded.

"My me drops, bitch!" one babbled.

"What?"

"She say she no have have any drops but she lying."

"And?"

Her bloodshot eyes frowned even deeper, she crossed her arms and then turned her back on me. "Well?" I said again.

She whirled around and kicked me in the head. I went out like a light.

I came to in the sick bay laying on a medic with an IV needle stuck in my arm and wearing an oxygen mask. My head hurt like hell.

Destiny and Tammy were there. I took off the mask and started to get up, but they pushed me back down. "Hold off, John, you should rest. The gurney said you had a slight concussion."

Gurney. That's what they call medics back on Earth. At least the boat's name made more sense than the Earth name, not like Port and Starboard and head.

"No I shouldn't," I said. "I should kick that cunt's ass and lock her up."

"The robots already did. They tased her," Tammy said. I thought, really? I didn't know they could do that. Why the hell can't they make decent coffee? Or patch a leak? Or even find one? And I remember seeing something on the news about the company researching ways to program some three "laws" some guy wrote about a few hundred years ago or so in fiction. Some sort of safety program.

"You two tased her," I said.

They looked at each other. "I did," Destiny said.

"Thank you," I replied.

"I'm sorry," Tammy said. "She should have had drops. You can't blame her, I missed her. It's my fault you're on that gurney, and I'm sorry. But if you're going to get mad at somebody, get mad at me, not her. And John, finish reading that book and fewer things like this will happen. If you'd read the rest of the book this one probably wouldn't have happened."

I sighed. "What's going to happen to them on Mars?" I asked.

"They think they're going to be prostituting, but they're going to be rehabilitated. The study of the brain and mind has really advanced in the last couple hundred years and these days we can undo much of the harm done to them in their lives. Many if not most drug addicts, not just droppers but people addicted to older drugs as well, even ancient drugs like the opiates, are mentally ill to begin with. Much of their illness comes from untreated trauma in their lives, and some are chemical imbalances from faulty gene sequences. These are the easiest, we simply balance the chemistry."

I didn't have a clue what "faulty gene sequences" are. It dawned on me that she didn't talk like a college professor around the whores like she did when none of the hookers were around.

She continued. "Cure their mental problems and it's a

lot easier for them to kick the drugs and lead a normal life.

"They used to think that the drugs caused the mental illness, and psychoactive drugs really can harm the mind. And they used to treat many mental illnesses with some of the same psychoactive drugs! But most of them are mentally ill to start with. Mental illness causes drug use far more often than drug use causes mental illness.

"When their five year contracts are up they won't be the same people. We hope they'll stay on Mars, Mars needs people badly. It has too many PhDs and too few less educated people; there are things that need to be done that don't require a higher education and it's a waste to have a research scientist doing without help for mundane things. There aren't even enough robots. There's such a shortage of robots and unskilled workers that sometimes scientists have to clean their own labs. Some restaurants have to have human cooks because robots are so scarce, usually the restaurant owner does the cooking him or herself. Only a very few Martian homes have robot cooks. Robot repair pays pretty good and needs no college, it's just a six week course. And they need people to build the robotic factories that manufacture robots, and they're building smelting plants. Mars really needs construction workers badly."

"Well," I said, "I think you'd have to be crazy to try any of that shit in the first place. So you conned them?"

"No, we said up front that addiction treatment was not only part of the deal but was the primary purpose, that's why the trip to Mars. These girls don't want to be addicts or prostitutes, that's just where life put them. But they worried about income; most of these girls know of no other way of making money. We're going to teach them how."

"Who's paying for all of this?" I asked. It sounded like I was the captain of a charity boat.

"The CEO of your company's daughter is a philanthropist. She's paying for it." She looked at Destiny. "Destiny works for them, too."

Destiny looked sheepish. "Look, John," she said, "you're not supposed to know any of this. So you don't know any of this, okay?"

"Okay," I said. Hell, I didn't care about Tammy but I sure hoped I didn't get Destiny in any trouble. That was the last thing I wanted. "I'll play ignorant," I said. I didn't know they were going to make me write this damned report.

The computer beeped and the readout said I could leave, so we started the walk home. Tammy went into her quarters and we continued on.

"*Ich habe keine Augentropfen*, bitch!" we heard while walking past the commons. God damned whores... We went in the commons. The fat blonde was there arguing with one of the Thai chicks. I have no idea what "*Ich habe keine Augentropfen*" means except yeah, I do, since after she said it she said "bitch". Sue, another Thai chick from someplace called Bong Chong; at least, the name of the place sounded like Bong Chong to me. I guess that's somewhere in Thailand, I don't know. Anyway, she usually pretty much kept to herself, but was trying to bum drops from the fat blonde woman, and she didn't speak hardly any English and no German at all and the German woman could speak English but didn't talk any Thai, so I don't know how they were communicating.

At any rate, Sue was out of drops like Lek had been. Damn. I called the other Thai chick's room. "Lek, could you please come to the commons? I need an interprepter." I didn't know that Tammy spoke fluent Thai.

This was the one chick who was arguing with the one who had attacked me, who had been trying to get drops from another woman. I think, anyway, I get them mixed up and I was still groggy from that kick in he head and wasn't sure which one kicked me. Anyway, it confuses the hell out of me, both with the same name. It sounds the same to me, anyway; one tried to show me how they were supposed to be pronounced but my western lips just won't move like that, and my western ears can't tell the difference.

91

"Okay, Joe, I be right there. Cost you some drops, though, okay?"

"I'll try but I can't promise."

"Try hard, Joe," she said threateningly.

"My me drops!" The other one said. "Meow drops!" I guess they're called "drops" in all languages. Wait... the German woman didn't say "drops", did she? She did say "bitch", though, but she does speak English real good, even though there's that heavy accent.

Damn, I hoped Lek hurried. "You'll get drops," I said. "Just be patient."

"Meow drops ticks in knee!"

"I'll see what's taking Lek," I lied. I was going to see someone who knew what the hell they was doing, and that was Doctor Winters, my expert on dropper whores who had pretended, and still did in front of everyone except Destiny and me, that she was one, too. I didn't know she didn't need an interpreter but I found out later she spoke Thai and a couple of other languages fluently. That's one damned smart woman, I'll tell you.

She was walking quickly toward me. "We have a prob..." I started.

"I know. My fault, sorry. I'll fix it. And John, *finish reading that damned book!*"

"I will..." I was going to tell her I'd been busy but hell, she was in the commons already. I shrugged and went back to my quarters to read some more.

The book said that when drops first came out, when they were doing drug trials, there was an angel tear addict who only weighed a hundred pounds that killed a musclebound three hundred pound championship freestyle fighter who was working as a bouncer in a redneck bar in Tennessee with her bare hands, and was eating the man's flesh. The crowd panicked when she killed the bouncer and a few people were trampled and one died. She ran out after the terrified crowd, screaming. Police were there by then.

The police's tasers had no effect on her at all, except to make her even more vicious. She put nine cops who were all trying to restrain her in the hospital while she had nine bullets in her before one shot hit her in the head and killed her.

Oh – you guys should put chapter ten from her book in this report, the whole thing will make a lot more sense that way. Chapter ten is a video of a drophead going through withdrawal. It's a hard video to watch. I'd rather I had just read about it, and I really don't like to read. I threw up watching it, and I have a strong stomach. I mean, Billie burning herself up didn't bother my belly. Well, maybe the stench turned my stomach a little but I didn't throw up.

But the woman in the video tore her own face off with her fingernails! It was horrible, and I puked and shut it off. How does Tammy study this kind of thing? I'm glad we had the noisy damned maid, the vomit stank and made me want to barf more.

I went in the head and rinsed my mouth and brushed my teeth. After my stomach quieted down I turned the book back on and they had one woman they called a "subject" in a straitjacket, locked in a padded room. Dead the next morning. Damn but that shit is nasty.

Destiny came in. "Are you okay, John?" she said with a worried look on her face. I guess I must have been a little pale.

"Yeah. Damn, how does Tammy do it?"

"Do what?"

"Study a Frankenstein monster. God," I said, "Worse than a Frankenstein monster. That book... Destiny, *a woman tore her own face off!* My God but that was the worst thing I've ever seen in my life!"

I didn't know that I'd see a whole lot worse than that, in the flesh, the ripped and torn and eaten flesh, before the trip was over.

She said "I read it. Why do you think I'm working for the charity? These poor women... the withdrawal from this drug is horrendous torture and they all die if they stop taking it. We're trying to find a cure. The problem is, we just can't tell on Earth because the drug is so easy to make there, because of Earth's exact gravity. A chemist could do it with a centrifuge on Mars, but a dropper couldn't. On Earth, we can get them through withdrawal but they go right back to using. So we're trying it where a dropper can't make drops, with the very best medical and psychological help there is.

"If we succeed," she continued, "we can not only rid Earth of its dropper problem but perhaps even populate Mars as well!"

I was doubtful but didn't say anything. It would be nice if they could pull it off, but I didn't think they would.

Uh, guys, I need to piss. Thanks. Be right back.

Where was I? Oh, Tammy's book. They were trying to make a female viagra and wound up with drops. The stupid scientists didn't see how dangerous and addictive they would be until after the drug trials.

It came out after the woman killed the prizefighter and put nine cops in the hospital arresting her, with bullets in her no less, before she was shot in the head that she was addicted to the chemical the scientists were testing, and was going through withdrawal when she killed the guy. She had been an experimental subject, whatever that is, but I gathered the scientists gave her the drugs.

Of course, they stopped the experiment right then and there, but the formula was already out, filed in the patent office. And it was really easy to make and the necessary chemicals were all common and available anywhere.

My fone and tablet went off at the same time. Fifteen minutes to decel.

"Gotta work, huh?" Destiny said.

"Yeah, you can cheer me up later. I gotta turn this tub around."

"Do we get zero G?" She asked. "Only a little," I said. I know what the book says is acceptable. I hate books.

Especially Tammy's. God but I hated reading Tammy's

fucking disgusting book.

Chapter Twenty

Reverse

I went into the pilot room, still haunted by the horrible, awful, terrible sight of a faceless woman, and strapped in. As I always do, I warned the cargo and passenger that we were going to zero gravity for a couple of minutes in a while and to strap down. The computers can give you a better idea of the maneuvers so I won't go into detail about that.

However, there was one thing that wasn't right: one of the computers disagreed with the other three about a reading. I never saw that happen before. I dropped to point zero nine gravity and trudged... bounded grudgingly might be a better way to put it, since we were at point zero nine gravity, to the remaining generator, which is what the computers disagreed about. At that low gravity I could just jump down there, but I didn't.

In all my years of driving these boats I've never seen the computers disagree about anything, so I was pretty worried. Especially since we only had one generator left; we could make it to Mars on batteries, but if we had to we'd be like Wild Bill and in danger from the pirates when we got close to Mars. That's where the pirates usually are, because that's when shipping is most vulnerable to them. We'd be later than we were already going to be, too, but compared to pirates late doesn't matter at all. Better late than dead.

But what was worse was if the computers died, we probably would, too. It ain't like I know calculus, and it would take a long time to get to us and the droppers would probably run out of drops.

The disagreeing computer was right, there was a tenth of a volt overvoltage occasionally going to engine seventeen, but a tenth of a volt wouldn't hurt anything. Hell, there are how many hundreds of thousands of volts going through each of those things? At how many amps? I shut number seventeen down anyway, and then went back to the pilot room, strapped in, got ready to maneuver and dropped the thrust to zero G.

The fone beeped. "John, Bill here. I got some bad news for you, old buddy. I picked up some radio traffic from pirates, and one of the boats you rained on had survivors. They're really, really pissed off at you, John. Be careful when you get close to Mars. Have all your weapons armed, not just as many as the book says but all of 'em. And if I was you I'd even have atomics ready. You should have heard them talking about you. There's a price on your head, John. Sorry to bring bad news, hope I see you on Mars, I'll buy you a beer. Kelly out."

Shit. God damn them pirates, I wish the company would build a few warships to rid the solar system of those God damned mother fucking sons of bitches. God damned bastards!

I got the boat turned around and went back to my apartment... sorry, "quarters". We had "normal" gravity again.

Destiny looked up from her tablet as I came in. "What's wrong, Johnnie?"

"Bill called," I said. "One of those damned pirate boats had survivors and now the pirates want my head. We're sure to be attacked when we get close to Mars."

Her eyes got wide. "Oh, my," she said, "Are we going to be okay?"

"Don't worry," I reassured her, worried myself. "Bill called the company when we tangled with them before. They're sending a huge armed convoy to escort us on the last leg where the pirates are, and escort Bill, too. Meanwhile we can still outrun and outmaneuver them with one generator. And we have arms ourselves. In fact, I'm getting a cup of coffee and then checking out our weapons and setting them up for arming so I can do it from the pilot room.

"Look, hon, don't mention pirates to anybody, okay? I'll get in trouble if you do. Strictly speaking I shouldn't even let you know."

"Don't worry, John, I won't."

"That generator itself is a weapon, even," I said. "I can make it spew gamma rays behind the boat and they'll be too sick to fight in minutes and dead in days. Honey, we're armed to the teeth. We have rail guns, lasers, EMP mines and rockets, other atomics..."

I got a cup of coffee. "Ugh," I said after taking a drink.

"Sorry," she said, "the robot made it."

"Nasty damned robots," I replied. "I'll make a fresh pot."

"What do you mean by 'other atomics'?"

"We have hydrogen bombs. Lots of 'em. You don't think the company would leave their property defenseless, do you? Once the weapons are armed they're automatic. Mark your targets and press a button and the computer does the shooting, and it never misses."

Damn, I didn't want to wait for a cup of coffee. Oh well. As the coffeepot gurgled I said "And please, remember, don't say anything about pirates to anybody, you don't know anything about it, okay? The company is strict about that, passengers and cargo aren't supposed to know about danger unless necessary. It's a gray area with you, captains are allowed to confide in spouses and we're a couple.

"I especially want the whores kept in the dark, they're the last ones I want to upset. I'm a lot more worried about them than I am about pirates."

She laughed. "you finished Tammy's book."

"Yeah," I said, "I did. Scariest book I ever read."

"You've read a lot of scary books?" she asked, grinning.

"No," I admitted, "I don't really like reading."

"That's too bad," she said. "Look how much help Tammy's book is to you."

"That damned book gives me nightmares! It's about

monsters!" I exclaimed, finally pouring my coffee.

"It might save your life," she said sternly.

"Yeah," I agreed. "I wish I'd read it before that first rock rain. I'd have known a little about the effect of lowered gravity on dropheads, although the book hardly said anything at all about that. I'm worried, they don't even like the half gee and as we gradually lower to Mars gravity... I need to talk to Tammy, I guess."

"You've been calling them dropheads lately."

"Got it from the dropheads themselves. Seems that a 'drophead' is an angel tear addict and a 'dropper' is anybody who uses them but isn't necessarily addicted to them. One of them said 'I ain't no drophead, bitch' to another one, but they're all dropheads. Some get addicted the first time they try it, according to Tammy's book."

"I know," she said, "I read it."

"Why didn't you tell me?"

"I thought you read the book."

"I should have. I should read more."

"Yeah, you should."

I finished my coffee. "I gotta get back to work."

She asked "want to watch a movie when you get back?"

"Sure," I said, "make it a funny one. One without any damned droppers."

"Old one then," she said. "Today's comedies all have droppers."

"Nothing funny about droppers," I growled. Damned whores... I was sure going to be glad when this trip was over. At least, if I lived through it. I mean, pirates were after me and I was hauling monsters.

Chapter Twenty One

Golf

"You've been practicing, boss." That was a private joke between the two of them; they were equal partners. Whoever won the golf game was called "boss" and whoever lost paid for lunch and drinks.

"Putting," the CEO replied. "I've Been practicing putting, that's where I'm weak at this game. First time I ever beat you, Charles."

"Well, I was a little off today. And you only beat me by one stroke," the president said. "That was a great hole three, you eagled that one."

"I got lucky on the initial drive. I usually put a ball or two in the water on that hole. Bartender, two beers. Guinness draft, please. Charles, you're paying for a change today! Oh, and bartender, a couple shots of your best Scotch, too."

Charles laughed. "Well, that was the deal. Maybe we should try some zero G golf sometime."

"Zero G? Damn, Charles, we're not twenty any more. That's a young man's sport. Besides, I hate space."

"Really? You run a travel and shipping company and hate space?"

"No, I love making money in it, I just hate traveling in it. You did pretty good on the second hole or I'd have done even better against you. How are we doing on the sabotage front?"

"Come on, Dewey, we're just starting. You can't just solve a complex problem like that in a few days, and Johnson only got the assignment this morning. Did you finish that report Knolls wrote?"

"No, I got sidetracked by the book Doctor Winters wrote that Knolls mentioned in his report. Damn, we need to check cargo closer, that book was horrible. I'm sure glad the charity sent Doctor Winters, it would have certainly been catastrophic otherwise.

"Then I read the report she made to her charity. I'll finish Knolls' report when we get back from 'lunch'."

"How did you get Doctor Winters' report? She works for the charity, not for us," the company president said.

The CEO smiled. "Don't be stupid, Charles. It's my daughter's charity and I'm one of its biggest contributors."

"So, how much of Knolls' report have you read?"

"Past where he saved her life. It's a good thing he didn't go by the book, she would have died if he did! Speaking of books, Charles, you have a terrible taste in literature. Knolls couldn't write his way out of a paper bag and you enjoyed it? Damn, man. I thought it was terrible. Awful grammar, run-on sentences..."

Charles shrugged. "At least it wasn't dry like all the other reports. We were sure lucky the charity sent Doctor Winters, Dewey."

"Yes, we were, like I said."

"Knolls was even luckier, and is probably glad he had her and the addicts, he'd have been a dead man, and probably Kelly as well. Nobody expected what happened."

The CEO asked "Have you talked to Human Resources to see about training a replacement for Knolls?"

"Of course. I hate to replace him, especially with a greenie. Some of the maneuvers and weapons use he displayed in his second encounter with the pirates should go into our training manuals. In fact, some of the things he did when he wasn't following the book ought to be in the regulations and training manuals. Knolls is really sharp."

"Yes, he was a damned good captain, but I haven't gotten that far in the report yet. The company will miss him."

"Well, I intend to try and talk him out of retirement."

"Good luck with that! I hear he wants to tend bar on Mars, maybe open his own bar. If you succeed you're the world's greatest salesman."

The president said "I'm taking the afternoon off today, Dewey. I want to be refreshed and rested for the board meeting tomorrow afternoon. Do you want to shoot another nine?"

"Sorry, Charles, I can't. I should have gotten back earlier, I want to finish reading Knolls' report, and I have a meeting with Richardson from engineering. I'm *that close* to firing that dumb son of a bitch. That was a hell of a boner he pulled, and I'm sure glad you brought the matter to my attention."

"Hell, if I hadn't we should have both been fired!" the president said, smiling, as if that was ever likely; between the two of them they owned sixty three percent of all company stock.

The CEO laughed. "Yeah," he agreed, "we should have been! Look, Charles, enjoy the afternoon and I'll see you tomorrow morning when we talk to the department heads. Like I said, I have to get going, I have a lot on my plate today."

"See you, Boss. Bartender, can I get another beer here?"

Chapter Twenty Two

Junk

I felt pretty good the next day when I woke up. Destiny was still asleep, so I started coffee, told the robot to make breakfast and *no robot coffee, damn it!* And took a shower.

Huh? Bacon, eggs, and hash browns for two. What? Turkey bacon, of course. Christ, do I look like I'm rich? What's wrong with you guys, anyway?

Destiny would be awake by the time I got out of the shower. Huh? Why? Over easy. Come on, guys! What difference does it make how the God damned eggs are cooked or whether it's ham or turkey bacon? I thought you said it didn't matter? You need to know what my turds looked like, too?

She was just waking up as I got dressed. "Hungry?" I asked. "I made coffee and the robots are making breakfast."

"I'll probably be hungry when my stomach wakes up. What time is it?"

"About seven thirty, we have a half hour before I have to go to work."

"Is the coffee done?"

"It should be by now, I started it before I got in the shower."

"Well, I guess I'll get up, then," she said grinning, and got up.

She put the news on the video... or is that "olds" since it's the same old shit? There was something on it about pirates, though. They had arrested thirty of them after a firefight on Earth, and fifty pirates and twenty policemen died. Hell, I just killed hundreds of the bastards and all I had to do was throw rocks at 'em. And only the bad guys died. Cops? Hah! You're better off fucking with cops than fucking with me. That is, if you're a pirate, anyway.

Stupid news.

Destiny and me wasn't paying much attention to it anyhow.

Five 'til eight I went to the pilot room to make sure we weren't going too fast or too slow or the wrong way and that the computers weren't arguing, and started my inspections.

There hadn't been any arguing coming from the computers but there was arguing coming from the commons, damn it. I stopped and called Destiny. "Hon, could you call Tammy and have her handle these crazy women?"

"Sure, what are they doing?"

"They act like they need drops."

"Okay, I'll call her."

I decided to inspect the commons last. A bunch of dangerous dropless dropheads was the last thing I needed. Tammy's damned book scared the hell out of me.

For once the cargo didn't give me any trouble in inspection at all; they were all asleep and the doorbells didn't even wake them up.

Odd, what with the commotion in the commons.

When I went into the passenger section there was a funny smell in number eighteen. Burning insulation and ozone, it smelled like. I got out fast and pulled out my fone; systems should have seen that and fixed it already.

"Computer, fire in number eighteen."

"There is no fire in cargo eighteen."

"PASSENGER eighteen you stupid computer!"

There was the muffled "crackle, wump" sound of an electrical explosion in number eighteen. Shit! "Computer," I said as alarms went off. "Report."

"Fire in passenger eighteen" it said as the door light started flashing red. "Fire suppression technologies in play."

Damned stupid computer. "Cause of fire?" It had

smelled like an electrical short circuit to me, ozone and burned plastic and it sounded like an electrical explosion. They don't make these boats near as good as they used to. This was the third damned fire on this ship! It wasn't a brand new boat, thank God, or the damned robots would talk. But the boats with three generators, the old ones that were built with one fission generator and got retrofitted with fusion power in addition to the original generator later, almost never had electrical problems. I hear when they used fission the most they could get out of them was a little more than half a gravity. I think we're the only company with fusions so far.

"Unknown at this time," the idiotic computer said. Stupid damned thing, something shorted out and a circuit breaker should have blown but didn't. Same as the port generator, it should have shut itself down before it caught fire and melted lots of the parts. I think the company needs better engineers.

I decided to investigate later. "Computer, do not repair until I've investigated the fire. Continue fire suppression and keep the door locked."

"Acknowledged," it typed on my fone. Why do them damned things talk like that? I'm glad my robots are old, I hate those damned new talking robots.

Well, except that the old ones catch fire sometimes. That's never any fun.

I went down all those damned stairs and inspected the good generator, the ion engines, and the messed up generator. One robot was working on engine one thirty two and I noted it in the log before trudging back up all those damned steps.

Back at Passenger eighteen the light was no longer flashing, so I went in. Yep, a burned up panel. I opened it, and it was fried; something had shorted. I logged it. A repair robot would come by and fix it shortly.

This shit didn't use to happen on old boats. The ones with three generators were built like brick shithouses, they almost never broke.

I went to the commons and finally inspected it. The commotion was over and it was nearly empty.

I went home and had a tuna salad sandwich and chips for lunch with Destiny. I was a little late because I'd been so busy and was starved.

"What was going on in the commons?" I asked.

"Thieves. You read Tammy's book, most of these girls had criminal parents and stealing is normal for them. Well, there were about fifty of them that had all their drops stolen and were in the commons accusing each other of stealing, when the thieves that had stolen them were all asleep. Tammy took care of it."

"I'm sure glad we have her," I said.

"Me too," she agreed. "Do you have to work this afternoon?"

"I hope not. Not unless something breaks or the droppers act up or pirates attack or..."

"Okay," she said laughing. "I get it. Want to watch something?"

"Sure. Pick something."

"How about..." she started before an alarm went off.

"You jinxed me," I said, grinning. "Damned dropheads!"

It was another fire, this time in passenger nineteen, right across the hall from where the earlier fire was. Why in the hell are unoccupied quarters powered? It don't make no sense. It's a fire hazard, especially the shitty way they build boats these days, I'm glad I didn't get a brand new one. I'll bet they're even worse than this one, and it's only ten years old. And the stupid robots would talk, too.

But it wasn't a real fire, just a drill, there only to waste my free time and annoy me. I have so damned many real emergencies that I don't need no stupid drills. The company's programmers are idiots.

I went back to watch videos with Destiny. I think it was called "The Untouchables"; it was about the nineteen twenties when beer was illegal. Boy, people are sure stupid.

106

We had steak and beans and slaw for dinner, then watched another movie, then we... Huh? I'm not sure what it was called, wild something I think. It was one of the old gray two dimensional movies. There were motorcycles in it, the old noisy kind that ran on some sort of liquid fuel rather than batteries. We didn't pay much attention, we got kind of occupied.

What? None of your God damned business!

Chapter Twenty Three

Animals

Destiny was already awake and dressed when I got up the next morning. I'm really glad she was there or I might have overslept.

"Are you going to sleep all day? Your breakfast is going to get cold. I'm eating," she said.

I groaned, rolled out of bed, put on a robe and followed her to the dining room. She'd made coffee and had the robots make French toast, bacon, and tater tots. I didn't feel like tater tots, though. "What time is it?" I asked.

She laughed. "You need a clock right there on the wall! Computer, what time is it?"

The damned talking table said "The time is seven twenty eight." Good, plenty of time. I finished eating and took a quick shower and started my morning chores about five minutes early. This time two of the computers disagreed with the other two. What the hell, I never saw them disagree before, ever, and here it happened twice on the same run!

Two said "systems were nominal", one said that engine sixty four was getting three volts too much and the other said number sixty four was two volts short. Oh, well, I was going to have to walk the stairs anyway, so I decided I'd get engine and generator inspections out of the way first, even though two or three volts was almost nothing when you're talking the voltages that go through those giant things. But I wasn't going to chance losing any engines or that last working generator if I could help it, let alone my computers. That's what really had me worried.

As I passed the commons Lek walked up, the one that talked English kind of okay.

"Captain Knolls?" she said, which kind of confused me for a second because the whores usually called me "Joe" even though they know my name is John.

"Lek?" I said, "how can I help?" I read Tammy's book, I didn't want to piss these dropheads off.

"Look, Captain, you surely know what not having drops do to us by now and I no can find dealer."

I almost said "I ain't got no drops, bitch" out of habit but I didn't. Instead I said "You're short of drops? Look, talk to..." Damn, I almost screwed up and gave Tammy away. Damn it, John!

"Uh," I continued. "...talk to me when this comes up, please! Lek, I finally get it. I do inspections and can confiscate..."

"No," she said, "It not me, It's Sparkle. She going to..." she hung her head. "Sun Dan, I really hate myself. I not human without drops! What has happened to me? But Sparkle need drops or she be dangerous wild animal and I no can find dealer and no have extra drops."

I really felt sorry for these women. I didn't think of them as whores any more, even though they never wore any clothes and I still called them that sometimes; life had really kicked their asses. Tammy's book had really opened my eyes. These poor women.

I walked down the hall and called Tammy on my fone, but she was already on it.

"Tammy, could you get some..."

"Drops to Sparkle?" she interrupted.

"Yeah. Is she..."

"She's okay. Now, anyway. But John, even though I knew, thanks. Please, if it comes up again call me, don't hesitate!"

"Jesus, Tammy," I said, "Of course I will, after I read your book I know how dangerous a dropless drophead is."

I finished walking down the hall to the stairs, then down that five damned flights of them. Most of this boat is engines. Second is generators, the generators take up a whole lot more space than quarters and storage combined, and storage is as big as passenger quarters and cargo pens and the commons and sick bay put together. Maybe bigger. Machine storage is above the generators, one flight down and about two stories high.

I checked number sixty four first, of course. It read normal. I almost logged that, but it suddenly dropped two volts, then immediately to a two and a half volt overvoltage, then normal again, really fast. Bill told me once that that usually meant a bad electrical connection, he's kind of a nerd.

It's good to know nerds like Bill. I was a little relieved, I had been worried that there was something wrong with my computers, and that would have really been some serious trouble. But it explained their disagreeing with each other. I shut sixty four down like the book says, plugged a repair robot into it in "diagnostic mode" then inspected the rest of them. I don't know why I have to check the port generator, since it's broke, but I do so I did.

Yep, still broke, no generator fairies on the boat, and no missing parts magically appeared.

The starboard generator was fine.

The damned alarm went off. Fire in cargo seven. I didn't know whether to cuss the damned dropheads or the damned stupid engineers who design shit that catches fire and have emergency drills in the middle of a real emergency.

I fucking hate it when there's an emergency upstairs when I'm downstairs. I have to *run* up those five damned flights of stairs. Yeah, we're at half gravity now but it goes down slow, after the first day you don't really notice it dropping. The droppers hadn't complained, except when it had sudden changes like when we sped up to beat the rocks. I'm just glad I didn't have to run up the stairs that day I was climbing around outside. Oh, wait, I did, didn't I?

110

Anyway, I wished we were at zero G, I could have made it to the top in seconds. But then, of course, the women would kill me.

The red light was flashing on cargo seven. "Computer, is there anybody in there?"

"Parse error, please rephrase the question."

God damned stupid computer. "Is cargo seven, uh, occupied?"

"Negative." That was a relief; not only does the company get pissed off when cargo was damaged, these weren't just cargo, they were people. Human beings.

At least, they were human when they had their drops. What Lek said was spooky, like one of those old horror movies Destiny likes, the really old two dimensional ones with werewolves and vampires and no colors. It put Tammy's book in a whole new light. I kind of shivered a little.

The flashing light stopped flashing and I went in. There was a burned up maid in the room. Hell, was it noon already?

Another burned up... wait, what was the number on that thing? R2? That's the same maid that burned up before. Whoever programs the robots that repair the other robots needs an ass kicking, or at least an ass chewing.

I pulled out my fone. "Computer, take R2 out of service until the maintenance when we get to Mars."

"Acknowledged," it replied. Another robot dragged it off to storage, and a third started noisily cleaning up the mess the fire had caused.

I went to the commons, which right now was a restaurant with robot waiters and robot cooks and bussbots and about a hundred naked women. I thought "I'm going to have to start inspecting cargo at lunch time so I don't have to talk to them." Not that these girls eat much, except the fat blonde with the thick German accent. They slept more than anything, never ate breakfast and not many ate supper. Except the blond German, who was always in there eating, it seemed like.

"Attention," I yelled. They ignored me, and the din continued. I stood on a table, pulled out my fone and addressed the PA, they can't ignore that.

"Attention, ladies, who lives in number seven?"

"That's Crystal," one of them said.

"Where is she?"

"I don't know. Oh, there she is," she said as a skinny red haired woman walked in.

"Where have you been?" I demanded, jumping off the table. "You're supposed to go to straight to the commons when your quarters catch fire."

"What?" she said, startled. "My quarters caught fire? I was in Leslie's cabin and got hungry. Is my stuff okay?"

What stuff? All these girls came with was the clothes on their backs, except Destiny and Tammy. Apparently they didn't have any use for them since they never wore them.

"Yeah," I said, "the only thing that burned was the maid."

"Good, I hate that noisy damned thing! Robot, I want a ham and cheese sandwich and a chocolate shake."

The computer said "Ham is not on the menu."

"Okay, how about a pork chop sandwich?"

"There are no pork products on the menu."

"Why not?"

"The only meat listed in the database is beef, mutton, venison, rabbit, squirrel, chicken, turkey, and duck."

"Yuck, I hate duck."

"There is no chef named Yuckeye Hade or recipe for a dish by that name listed in the database."

"Stupid computer. Give me a Reuben and a chocolate shake."

"Affirmative."

"Fuck off, you stupid computer," she said. "Waiting for input," it said. She kept arguing with the computer. I went to continue inspecting the ship.

I finished inspection by one thirty and was starved by

then. Destiny called. "Where are you? I'm starved," she said. "I'm about ready to eat without you."

"Walking back to our apartment," I said. Oh, shut up you two, that's what I said. I told you I don't want to hear any of that "professional" shit, I ain't no God damned professional, I ain't went to college. Anyway, I said "Go ahead and have the robot start cooking, I don't care what."

We had pizza and beer and watched an ancient comedy, a western called "Blazing Saddles", and I didn't understand a lot of it, but some parts were really funny. Destiny thought the whole movie was hilarious, and told me to read some history.

We had steak and deep fried onion rings and baked potato for dinner and watched some new holo and I didn't understand a bit of it, it didn't make any sense at all.

I fell asleep on the couch. Destiny woke me up and I went to bed.

Chapter Twenty Four

Engineering

The company's co-founder, largest stockholder, and CEO put the report down, greatly annoyed. This was certainly not his best day, good golf game aside. He'd spent way too much time on the golf course and only had time for a little more of Knolls' report, and now he had to chew out that incredibly stupid Chief Technical Officer, who was knocking on his door and in danger of losing his job. This could have crippled the company. "Come in," the CEO said.

It seemed the company he and Charles had practically built from scratch was falling apart. God damn it, quality was deteriorating badly, and he was starting to think he needed a new head engineer.

"Talk to me, Gene," he said as the CTO entered.

"Sir?"

God damn it, he thought. He opened a folder and handed an old fashioned piece of printed paper to the engineer. "I'm talking about this schematic wiring diagram. How in the hell did this happen, and why was it spotted by someone who wasn't even an engineer, let alone not an electrical engineer?"

Richardson said "I honestly don't know, sir."

"Your teams are getting really sloppy, Richardson. This has been built into ten ships already and they're all going to have to be rewired because engineering screwed up on the schematics. How in the hell could your team miss this? How the hell could *you* miss it? You have a master's degree in electrical engineering, man! An *intern* discovered it! And he wasn't even an engineering student, he was just an electronics hobbyist."

Richardson stared at his shoes. The CEO continued. "If these ships had been operational a lot of people would have died and it would have caused the company great financial hardship; we're self-insured. One more mistake like this and you're fired, Richardson, and I'll get someone competent.

"Now tell me, who programmed our robots to make coffee?"

"Sir?"

"Robot," Mister Green said, "Make this man a cup of coffee. Richardson, I got a report from a ship's captain complaining about the coffee, so I had a brand new one of our ship's coffee robots sent here to check, straight from the factory. He's right, this is the worst coffee I've ever tasted."

"Well, sir, I don't like coffee myself, I had Larry Jones program it."

"Why in the hell didn't you test it? That's the kind of sloppiness I'm talking about."

"We did do chemical tests, sir..."

"But you never thought of having anyone who actually drinks coffee try it? Look, Richardson, I'll be blunt: again, you're on the verge of losing your job. We have paying customers booking passage on our ships and they don't expect to make their own coffee and they expect the coffee they're served to be good coffee. I want a program for the coffeebots to make not just drinkable coffee, which this isn't, and not just good coffee, but great coffee. I want the program in a week and a demonstration in two weeks and updates sent to all the coffee robots as soon as it's tested, and by that I mean by a group of people who enjoy coffee, not a bunch of chemists. Put Jones on a project he's good at. This is unacceptable. Find someone who likes coffee to do it. Am I understood, Richardson?"

"Yes sir."

"And I want you to weed out the incompetents in your

shop. This sloppiness is inexcusable."

"Sir, the union..."

"Tell the union that if they give you any trouble there won't be a new contract, I'll replace every engineer and programmer in the shop as soon as the contract expires. The union is supposed to give us quality employees, and it doesn't look to me like we're getting them or that schematic wouldn't have been erroneous.

"This is your last chance. One more screw up and your career is over, Richardson. Now get out of here and get back to work, I have a report to finish reading."

After Richardson left, he buzzed his secretary. "Get Human Resources on the fone. And I don't want to take any calls unless it's the company president, my wife, kids, or an emergency after I talk to Human Resources." He drummed his fingers for a few seconds and the fone buzzed again. It was the company president.

"What's up, Charles?"

"Have you tasted our robots' coffee, Dewey? I was curious after reading Knolls' report. That's the nastiest coffee I ever drank, and I was in the Army."

"Yes, I did, and Richardson got a good ass chewing for it and for the mess your intern discovered. I threatened to fire him, and I might still after that botched wiring diagram. And his might not be the only head to roll, Knolls' report was an eye opener. You were right, it's invaluable. I want reports from all the captains after each run from now on."

"So do I, I've already ordered it. I'm leaving for Mars tomorrow on whatever of our first class passenger boats can get me there the fastest right after the meetings. I wish I could skip the board meeting.

"I'm especially worried about engineering, that's our most important function. I'm not too happy about financial, either. How did we let this slip past us, Dewey?"

"Hell if I know, Charles. Both of us are going to have to be more vigilant. We have an awful lot of work ahead of us.

Look, I have to finish reading this report. I may not finish it this afternoon so I want you to mostly take charge in the meeting, since you've read the whole thing and have more information. I'll see you in the morning. Goodbye."

"See you, Dewey."

He hung up and Human Resources buzzed. "We're probably going to need a new engineer, Larry," he said. "I want the best and he'd damned well better not be a criminal. I'm not sure what specialty, but get the ball rolling. I'll call when I know what kind of engineer we need."

He started reading again.

Chapter Twenty Five

Ease

I guess Destiny had stayed up and read or something. I woke up about six, wondering what time I'd fallen asleep on that couch, it must have been pretty early. I started coffee and was glad the robots were almost as good at cooking as they were bad at making coffee, because I didn't even feel like making coffee, let alone cooking. Well, they cook all right unless it had to do with barbecue sauce, and who has barbecue in space? Especially for breakfast?

Or pork, I remembered. I don't eat pork, it's been way too damned expensive for the last half century or more, way before I was born, and I like beef and chicken better, anyway.

But George Wilson, one of our guys who hauls first class passengers, eats it sometimes. The company has pork on the first class boats and he tells me the pork is as bad as the coffee. Odd that they cook bacon pretty good, but all you have to do with bacon is microwave it. The robots would have to be dumber than they already are to mess bacon up. Besides, only rich people eat pork bacon, normal people have turkey bacon and you cook them both the same way. I had a pork bacon sandwich with lettuce and tomato in a restaurant once and couldn't tell the difference. Except for the size of the bill, that was a damned expensive sandwich!

But that one trip I was hauling frozen pork to that big science station in orbit around Venus I had plenty of pork. Too much damned pork. Especially since I can't cook pork much better than the damned robots can. Yeah, my parents taught me to cook when I was a kid, but we were poor. We had to print everything out and we damned sure couldn't afford a luxury like cookbots or pork.

I was twenty five before I ate my first ham and cheese sandwich, as a treat to myself on my birthday. I didn't see what all the fuss was about, I thought thin sliced turkey was better, and a hell of a lot cheaper...

Huh? Oh, sorry, my mind kind of wandered. Anyway, while coffee was perking and the robots were making breakfast and Destiny was sleeping I took my shower and got dressed.

The smell of decent coffee that robots can't make must have woke Destiny up, because she walked in as I was pouring the first cup. I handed it to her, said "Good morning, sweetheart," and poured a cup for myself and kissed her. "Hungry?" I asked as I sat down. "I had the robot make waffles and sausage."

"Sausage? You have pork?"

I laughed. "Of course not, it's beef sausage. The company sure isn't going to pay for pork unless there's rich passengers traveling first class. And I damned sure can't afford it on a captain's wages."

"That's too bad," she said, "I love pork sausage but it's way too expensive to eat very often, I feel guilty when I do eat pork. Too frugal, I guess. I usually just eat it on my birthday for breakfast."

"I never ate any," I said. She switched the video on and we watched the "news" while we ate. There was one interesting item about a robot probe that was on its way to Alpha and Proxima Centauri at five gravities thrust, though. I wonder how fast that thing would be going by the time it was halfway there? Compared to Proxima, Neptune's right next door, and it's a long way off, even from Mars! It was already months ahead of its telemetry, and no, I don't know what "telemetry" is but that's what they said on the news. It sounded impressive to me, anyway. They said once it got there it would be four years before any data about those stars came back. Four years, that's a hell of a long way off.

It was almost eight so I kissed Destiny again and went to the pilot room. Everything was normal, so I started my inspections. It would be a light day, since I didn't have to inspect quarters. I still had a hell of a lot of ion engines to check out, though.

After the generator had blown out I'd reduced power to a third of the engines, and shut down engine twenty four, the one I'd made sputter when I'd killed all them damned pirates in the rock storm, and sixty four and seventeen, the ones with the funny voltages, were completely offline too.

I plugged robots into all three of them and had them do a "twenty four hour diagnostic" which is what they tell me the robots do when you plug them in like that. I'd see the results tomorrow. I might need those motors when we were closer to Mars and pirates were more likely.

I climbed up the five damned flights of stairs, and walked past the commons on my way home. The German woman was in there eating, as usual, and four more were playing cards. I wondered what they were gambling for... oh hell, I'm a dumbass, they were gambling for drops, of course. What else would they be playing for? I pretended not to notice and went home.

Destiny was reading, so I got a cup of coffee and started to sit down. "That's nasty robot coffee," she warned.

I poured it down the drain, rinsed out my cup and the pot and started a new pot. I had the robot make roast beef sandwiches, and we ate them when the robot finished. Destiny turned on the video to watch an old Western and put her tablet down when it started. I asked what she was reading.

She grinned. "A history of fones. I was reading an old historical novel about a nineteen thirties prison where they executed criminals by electrocuting them. Creepy book, but hard to understand in places, I have to look stuff up to see what the author is talking about. Like back then 'fone' was spelled with a P H instead of an F, I guess it was pronounced 'pone'. And they weren't really fones, they only did speech and they were all wired together, either attached to a wall or by a wire that went into the wall. Fones, or 'pones' as it was spelled then, didn't have radios or batteries or computers in them. There wasn't even any such thing as a computer that existed in the nineteen thirties!

"That prison book was creepy, I haven't finished it yet. Barbaric back then."

I asked "What are you putting on?"

"An old western with that one guy from *Rawhide*, called *The Outlaw Josey Wales*," she answered, and added "I haven't seen it yet," which surprised me. She's the one that got me liking these old westerns. I said "There's a movie listed that says it's about a nineteen thirties prison, I wonder if it could be from that book you're reading?"

"Probably not," she said, "but anyway the movies are never faithful to the books and usually aren't nearly as good."

That was a long movie, but it was a really good one. When it was finished, Destiny asked "Are you hungry?"

"I could eat."

She told the robot to cook a pizza and bring us some beers, and we drank our coffee while the pizza was baking.

When the pizza was done we watched a funny old movie called "Smokey and the Bandit".

We went to bed after it was over. Well, after cuddling and listening to music for quite a while...

Chapter Twenty Six

Heads

"Good morning, Mister Green," the company president said as he entered the room.

"Good morning, Mister Osbourne.

"Gentlemen and ladies, I had a particularly trying day yesterday, as a few of you know," the CEO said, looking at his chiefs of engineering, financial, and scheduling sitting in the small crowd of department heads. "We have some serious problems in the company and it lands squarely in your laps. Folks, we're getting complacent and sloppy and it stops right here and right now or heads are going to roll.

"If any of you think some of your employees are less than excellent, reassign them to something they're good at or get rid of them.

"Mister Osbourne has a few words to say about a few of the problems we're having, and some possible solutions to some of those problems. Mister Osbourne?"

"Thank you, Mister Green. Ladies and gentlemen, we have a severe quality control problem lately. Human Resources hired a saboteur who was employed by pirates to work in the shipyards in orbit around Mars, and it almost cost us a ship, a man, cargo, and our shipping fees for that load. That is unacceptable, we do *not* hire pirates. Ever. It had better not happen again, or Mr. Griffins won't be the only one turning in his resignation.

"I looked into the matter myself, and the saboteur should never have been able to pass a background check to begin with. The man should have never been hired in the first place. He was found guilty of misdemeanor retail theft and was fined for it when he was younger. We do *not* hire thieves or any other criminals, period. Any criminal record at all, no matter how minor, and I'm not talking traffic tickets here, use some judgment, that's what you're being paid for after all, is not suitable for employment at this shipping and travel company.

"I want everyone's records checked. If we have any felons on the payroll I want them terminated immediately; our contracts with the unions gives us the right. Anyone with a misdemeanor I want transferred to somewhere where they can't cause mischief, and that means they're not to be anywhere near one of our ships or near anything that goes into their construction or operation. If they do anything that the contract says we can fire them for, terminate them immediately.

"Mister Johnson suggested this to me, and I agree with him. He's still looking for and looking into other measures, but he's only been on the problem since yesterday.

"But what's just as bad and possibly even worse is you people are assigning the wrong people to the wrong teams, and you're not communicating with each other and neither are the teams. Our clients pay a lot of money to ride our transportation and they don't expect bad coffee and they don't expect to have to make their own. It was sheer stupidity to assign a programmer who doesn't even drink coffee to program robots that make coffee. You wouldn't assign a Jewish or Muslim person to program a cook to prepare pork, or an American to program it to cook dog."

Larry Griffins, head of both Finance and Human Resources, went pale and said "Sir, we can't discriminate against a person on the basis of religion or national origin."

"Of course you can't," the president said, "but you can discriminate on the basis of competence. Don't assign a person to a project that he or she would not want to sample the end result of him or her self.

"No one is competent in building a repair robot unless

he or she can repair a robot him or herself. Look, Mister Richardson, your engineers and programmers are nerds. If someone likes fixing stuff in his spare time as a hobby, have him program repair robots, not the guy who loves to cook and hates to work on a machine. If you're competent and working on something you love, you'll create excellence. If you hate what you're doing you're going to hate the work and the best work you do will never be better than mediocre. Do you think a guy who doesn't like coffee wants to program a robot to make coffee? Do you think a Jewish person wants to program a cook to prepare pork? He would have stern religious objections. Just ask your staff what they want to work on. Come on, people, this isn't theoretical physics.

"It isn't just Richardson," the president said. "I dug up similar sloppiness, incompetence, and downright stupidity in all the departments, every single one of them. Ladies and gentlemen, you're becoming complacent and I'm simply not going to tolerate it from any of you.

"And *talk* to each other! We need far better commun-ications between departments. We could have saved ourselves a lot of money and our passengers a lot of time and trouble if scheduling had been talking to orbital instead of just giving them schedules. There's probably a whole lot more money to be saved, as well. Mister Griffins, you, especially, need to listen to the other heads. Folks, if you or any of your people have ideas for saving money or for the company to earn larger profits, call Mister Griffins. If he doesn't listen, email me or Mister Green, or call Mister Johnson if neither Mister Green or I are available.

"From now on, all of our ships' captains will be making a report after each run. I want all of you to read those reports when they come in; Captain Knolls' report is in your in-box now. Read it when this meeting is over. You should expect Captain Kelly's and Captain Ramos' in a day or two, next Monday at the latest. Like I said, you need to listen to other people. Nobody knows what improvements we can make to our shipping and transportation systems better than our ships' captains, so when I say read them, I mean *read* them. If a captain has a problem, you have an even bigger problem.

"We are the number one shipping and transportation company in the solar system and we're *not* going to let the other transportation companies catch up to us.

"I want a progress report from each one of you in one week, and I'd better see results or someone's going to be updating their résumés.

"This meeting is adjourned. Now get to work, you have your work cut out for you and you have a lot of it to do."

The president and CEO sat there silently until the last of the department heads left the room.

The president said "You know, Dewey, I haven't been in space in fifteen years, way back when we still used fusion generators on most of our boats and a lot of captains still needed degrees, before we made transportation prices drop and profits rise. I'm visiting Mars for a weekend to have a look at our repair facilities there."

"Yes, you mentioned that yesterday and I agree. We haven't knuckled down and gotten our hands dirty in quite a while. I think I'll visit the various departments tomorrow, surprise all of them. Well," he said standing up, "I have a report to finish reading, so I'm getting back to the office. I'll see you at the board meeting this afternoon."

"Sorry, Dewey, I have to miss the board meeting. My flight takes off in twenty minutes, but I'll be there by teleconference."

"Well, okay, I'll see you when you get back."

Johnson was waiting for him outside his offfice when he arrived. "What's up, Mark?" the CEO asked.

"I think we need to split security into a different unit."

Green sighed. "Come on in." It looked like he wasn't going to be able to read any more of the report today.

Chapter Twenty Seven

Movies

Destiny and me woke up at the same time the next morning. We cuddled a while, made love again, then started the coffee pot and took a shower together while the robots made us steak and cheese omelettes and toast and hash browns for breakfast.

Destiny said that when space travel first started way back in the nineteen sixties, it was a tradition that American astronauts had steak and eggs in the morning of liftoff, because all they had to eat in space was really crappy. I guess back then, eggs and steak was like pork or something is now, I don't know.

She put on the news. There was something about a problem in one of the company's boat factories; some machinery had something wrong with it and killed a guy. I sure took notice of that! They didn't really have much information about it, though. They said something about trying to build in safety laws into the robots' programming. I think I heard about something like that once or twice before.

Astronauts and their expensive breakfast made me think of the pork sausage Destiny had mentioned, and something occurred to me. "You can afford pork but it makes you feel guilty? I didn't know astronomy teachers made that much money. Pork is really expensive!"

"We don't," she said. "I should have told you, I don't just work for the charity, it's my charity. I started it and I run it."

"What?"

"Sorry, I never give my money any thought, I was born into it. My dad's Dewey Green."

I almost fell out of my chair. "Your... dad..." I was almost speechless. "Uh, your dad's my CEO? *That* Dewey Green? No shit?"

"Does it matter?"

"I don't know," I said. I was dumbfounded. "I can't support a CEO's daughter on a boat captain's pay!"

"You don't have to, silly, I pay my own way. Didn't you say you were going to retire and live on Mars with me anyway? Didn't you say you wanted to tend bar?"

"Well, yeah, but bartenders don't make much money either."

"No, but bar owners do. At least successful ones, you'll have to take some business classes on Mars, of course."

"I was going to go to college anyway, can't have a high school grad married to a PhD. What's your dad going to think?"

"It doesn't matter, he has no say. I'm not dependent on him and I won't be dependent on anyone. I got my endowment when I was twenty one and invested it. I have more money that he does, even."

"Holy shit," I said. "I would have thought I'd have heard of you, being the daughter of the CEO of the solar system's biggest shipping company and head of a charity and all that."

"I keep a low profile, and so does the charity. I don't want to be famous for anything but astronomy. That's why I'm going to Mars, there's a new kind of telescope I want to build there. Computer," she said, "what time is it?"

"The present time is seven fifty eight."

"Oh shit," I said, running to the pilot room.

Except for a slight course correction everything was fine, and that only took a minute. The computers do the work, I just make sure they all agree with each other and the readings are what they're supposed to be.

The commons only had the fat blonde in it. These girls

127

almost never ate breakfast, except for the blonde German woman. She was always in there eating, it seemed. Inspection was easy.

Cargo was easy for a change, too. Every single one was asleep, which was a relief. Tammy was keeping the animals under control and even keeping them human, apparently.

It was the passenger section that was a pain – R15 caught fire. Why in the hell are robots programmed to clean unoccupied quarters? Rooms that are never occupied shouldn't even have any air in them. Air is a fire hazard!

Anyway, there was nothing I had to do except log it. Another maid would come by to clean the mess after another robot dragged it off and repaired it. I thought of something, then thought better of it. I almost told the computer not to use parts cannibalized from other broken machines, but at this rate we would run out of maids. And probably other robots as well.

The sick bay was empty but I had to inspect it anyway, mostly to make sure its drugs were all secure, especially with all these drug addicts on board. Since there was nobody sick or hurt right now it didn't take any time at all.

Now it was time for my daily exercise routine, my five flights of stairs down to the engines and generators, and my long walk from one generator to the other, stopping at all those huge ion rocket motors.

All the engines and the lone working generator checked out and there weren't even any robots working on any of them except seventeen, twenty four, and sixty four so I was done early for a change. I was glad of it, as busy as I'd been lately I could use some time off. I trudged up the five damned flights of stairs and walked back to my quarters.

Destiny was reading as I walked in. "Johnie! You're home early!"

"Easy day for once. Computer, what time is it?"

The stupid table said "The present time is eleven thirteen."

"Want to eat lunch early and watch something?" Destiny asked.

"Sure," I said, and grinned. "Ham sandwiches?"

She laughed. "Yeah, with pork bacon and a side of caviar and truffles and a hundred year old bottle of French wine to go with it! How about a cheeseburger and shike?"

"How about a pizza and beer again," I suggested.

"Well, we did just have it last night but it still sounds good to me. Computer, a medium supreme pizza and two beers. We can eat it while we're watching. What do you feel like?"

I didn't care. "I don't know, pick something."

She put *Spaghetti* on. Huh? It's an old science fiction comedy from the first part of the twenty second century about a normal man in a world of incredibly stupid people. Destiny said it was one of the last two dimensional movies, holograms were finally getting cheap enough to produce for them to start being popular.

When that was over we watched some short old gray movie about international spies, Uncle something, I don't really remember the name.

We had spaghetti and meatballs and garlic bread for dinner and put on a modern holo, a really bad holographic recreation of one of the old westerns. It sucked. She shut it off after fifteen minutes and said "We should watch a spaghetti western."

"Huh?" I said. "What's a 'spaghetti western'?"

She said that a "spaghetti western" was a movie about the ancient American west that was filmed in Italy. No, I don't know why where a movie was made would matter, either.

Instead of a spaghetti western she put on an old two dimensional shades of gray horror *comedy*. Huh? No, I never heard of a horror comedy before either, but it was about the Frankenstein monster and it was hilarious. Destiny said the movie studio had balked at its not having colors, but they were making fun of the horror movies from fifty years earlier when none of them had colors.

When it was over we shut it off, put on some music, cuddled a while, and went to bed.

Huh? None of your damned business! Assholes...

Chapter Twenty Eight

Resignation

He'd only read a little more of the report when he laid the tablet down and grabbed the fone and called his secretary. "Book a first class flight to Mars as soon as you can get me there," he said. "And I don't mean the next one to take off, I mean the one that will get me there at the earliest time on the earliest date. Tell orbital I want Earth-normal gravity the entire trip."

He composed a letter to his daughter. "Dear Destiny," it said, "I wish you'd stay in touch. I'm in the middle of reading your fiancée's report and I see you're getting married. Please wait until I get there, I want to give my daughter away :)

"Love, Dad"

After he sent the electronic letter, a message from the company president came in.

"Dewey, I just now fired that idiot Richardson over email. That moron must have had a devout Jewish Rabbi to program the robots to cook pork, because I just had barbecued pork steaks on this ship and they were even worse than the coffee.

"The ship's captain is excellent, from what I can tell as a random traveler. You know I went under an assumed name. Well, no sooner had the robot brought me coffee and I'd taken a sip of the nasty brew when the captain himself brought a pot of very good coffee in and apologized for the robot coffee. He said he made coffee for all his passengers, even when he was flying cargo class passengers, even Martian prisoners being transported to Earth. At least some of our people are doing a good job, even above and beyond. Captain Muñoz said that all the first class captains were doing it, and even most cargo captains, and that there was even one guy named 'Tex' running one of our ships that made barbecued pork for his passengers. Steaks, ribs, chops, Muñoz said that Texas is famous for barbecue. I understand that the Australians are pretty crazy about barbecue, too. Muñoz said than none of the robot barbecue was any good.

"Anyway, I wish you'd talk to Engineering and promote someone as chief. See you when I get back to Earth."

The CEO sent a memo to all engineering staff.

TO: Engineering Staff
FROM: Dewey Green, CEO
SUBJECT: New Chief

Staff, your chief has tendered his resignation effective immediately and I am looking for his replacement. I want my engineers to be productive, and you're more productive when you enjoy your assignments. I want my engineers to be happy, to enjoy your jobs.

With that in mind, please reply with answers to the following questions, and let none of the answers be your own name.

1. Who do you consider to be our best engineer, and why?

2. Who would you most want to be chief engineer, and why?

3. Who would you consider to be our worst engineer, and why?

4, Who would you want least to be our chief engineer, and why?

5. Which of our engineers has the best people skills?

I expect a reply in one hour and will expect all of you to be in conference room three in two hours.

He poured a cup of coffee and started to call Human Resources, but then thought better of it. He would call them after he chose a new chief, so he would know which engineering specialty they would be hiring.

He picked up the tablet and started reading again.

Chapter Twenty Nine

Walking

I was almost late for my eight o'clock visit to the pilot room, and only had time to grab a robe. I didn't even have time to grab coffee, let alone a shower and breakfast. We shouldn't have watched that last movie, I guess. Well, inspections would be a little late today. I grimaced, and ordered a cup of coffee from the computer. Those robots must use instant coffee rather than perking it, because it tastes really nasty but they get a cup to you in no time, even though it seems like forever when you really need a cup of it. It takes at least fifteen minutes for my pot to make coffee.

It was nasty, but it was coffee, or an almost not unreasonable substitute for coffee, and I needed coffee. At least it would make me more alert. With all those damned drug addicts on board I needed coffee!

It looked like today wasn't going to be nearly as easy as yesterday. There was a slight course correction and engine sixty three had a minor undervoltage. I shut it down from the pilot room as Destiny came in with a cup of good coffee that the stupid robots can't make; she must have gotten up right after I did.

"Thanks," I said. "How late were we up last night? I almost didn't make it here on time."

She laughed. "I don't know, that last movie seemed like it was pretty long, and we cuddled longer than usual after it was over, too. Want some breakfast?"

"Sure," I said. She ordered the robot to make scrambled eggs and bacon and had a little fun with the computer, asking for pork bacon, and toast, and drank coffee with me as I finished up in the pilot room.

I got dressed and we ate a quick breakfast. My morning shower would have to wait today, engine inspections were more important than a shower so it was first. The robot plugged into sixty four had repaired it, so I unplugged the robot from it and restarted it and plugged the robot into number sixty three.

Robots were still working on engines seventeen and twenty three. Twenty three had two different kinds of robots working on it, so I logged that.

The port generator was still broke, of course, but other than being broke and completely useless it was fine. The starboard generator was in good shape, too.

Despite having a nasty first half cup of coffee and almost being late to work I was in a pretty good mood. I decided to let the girls who were confined out as long as they promised to be good... hah, like that promise meant anything. But like Tammy had said, these girls couldn't help themselves any more than a house cat can help its clawing your furniture or a dog can help itself from chewing up your slippers. They're animals.

I walked up all those damned stairs and headed home. As I was walking down the hall I ran across Lek and Billie.

Billie was actually civil, thanking me for letting her out and apologizing for the mutiny, but what was even more amazing was that Lek was actually clothed! I complimented her on the dress. "Thank you," she said, "I ashamed. I no want act like animal even though I am one."

That was a pretty good sign, according to Tammy's book. I was in an even better mood.

There were three girls whose names I could never remember, the fat German blonde and the skinny French redhead and a more normal sized Canadian woman with green hair, in the commons. Why her hair was green I had no idea; weird hair colors were a fad a few hundred years ago but were way out of style these days. Might as well have tattoos, those things were popular a few hundred years ago too but nobody had them these days. Maybe the weird hair color fad was coming back? What's next, nose rings? Those people back in the first part of the twenty first century were crazy.

The redhead and the blonde were eating, and the woman with the green hair was drinking something pink.

I could finally take a shower and eat; I was starved. Destiny had the robots make hoagies and potato splitters for lunch while I took my shower and put on clean clothes. The noisy maid was cleaning as we ate our sandwiches.

We took glasses of shike to the living room and watched an episode of *Rawhide*. When it was finished Destiny said "I think I'll take a walk, want to come along?"

"Sure," I replied. "Cabin fever?"

"Yeah, a little," she said.

Tammy was in the commons by herself with a tablet and stylus as we went past, so we decided to have another shike. "Working?" Destiny asked.

Tammy looked around furtively, making sure there were no droppers, and said "Yes, I'm writing a paper on the effects of low gravity on droppers, I'm really learning a lot on this trip. We only had a very little bit of data on that aspect of their addiction, so this is some important research. What are you guys up to?"

"Just going for a walk," Destiny said. "I haven't been getting enough exercise lately and I seem to be tired all the time. I might even walk down a few flights of stairs."

"I'm not," I said. "I get enough damned stairs every day. Tammy, Lek was actually wearing clothes this morning!"

"Really? Which one?"

"The one that talks English okay, the only Thai on board that does. I think she's the one that knocked me out."

"That's great!" she exclaimed, beaming. "I'll have a gurney examine her, maybe I can get that kind of progress from all of them, or at least more of them."

"Well, I don't know," I said, "she said she's ashamed that she's an animal."

"Excellent!" she said, and furiously scribbled something in her tablet with its stylus. I pulled out my fone. "Computer," I said, "send a medic to the commons and give Doctor Winters complete access and command control to it."

We went back to our walk, passing a few naked droppers as we went. By the time we got to the stairwell Destiny said she changed her mind about climbing stairs, so we went back to my quarters and watched some ancient two dimensional movie called "Dumbo" that had no actors, just colored moving drawings.

Destiny said that a century ago all movies were like that, except the drawings were done inside a computer and looked like they were real people and buildings and stuff... or almost. Now days only low budget B movies are made inside computers, they've gone back to using actors and sets and props again when they make real movies.

We had some kind of Mexican dish for dinner. I don't know what it was called, but I didn't care too much for it, it was way too spicy. It made my eyes water and my mouth felt like it was hot enough to blister.

We watched a really short but funny ancient movie about four college professors and their dumb blonde neighbor who wants to be an actor, then a beautiful old fantasy called "Lord of the Rings," or at least the first part – it had been taken from an old book that was written in three long parts.

Then we cuddled to some classical music and went to bed. And no, it's still none of your damned business.

Chapter Thirty

Kowalski

The CEO's fone buzzed; it was time to look over the papers from the engineering staff, then meet them in the engineering department. He pulled them up on his tablet.

Most of the answers to his queries were interesting and original. He noted that every single one of his engineers rated Robertson as the worst engineer in the shop, regardless of their own engineering specialty, and the one they least wanted to be chief.

He decided to promote Ron Kowalski to chief of engineering. His masters degree was in engineering, of course, but his minor as an undergrad had been psychology, and he was well liked by the rest of the staff. For the chief, this was even more important than his expertise at engineering, since he would be good at communicating with the other departments as well. Also, most of the staff wanted him as chief.

He called Human Resources. "Hello, Larry? We're going to need a new engineer like I told you we might. Yes, we'll need an electrical engineer. I want the best, okay? Thanks." Like Richardson, Kowalski was an electrical engineer.

He called Kowalski to his office, and once Kowalski got there Green said "Good morning, Mister Kowalski, please have a seat. Coffee?"

"Uh, yes sir, as long as it isn't robot coffee. Thank you, sir." Green's assistant gave Kowalski a cup. The CEO said "Congratulations, Mister Kowalski, I'm making you the new department head."

Kowalski looked startled. "Me? Sir, I'm no good at all at

bureaucrat stuff. I'm an engineer!"

"That makes you perfect for the job," Green replied. "This organization has way too much bureaucracy as it is, a bureaucrat would add even more. Bad for productivity. That was one of Mister Robertson's worse traits, he was a born bureaucrat, paying too much attention to the book but not able to pay much attention to people at all.

"It's important that your programmers and engineers are developing machines and systems in an area they know and like."

"Yes, sir," Kowalski replied, "that was our biggest complaint; Mister Robertson always seemed to give us the jobs we hated and were worst at. I couldn't believe he had Mohamed Nisbah program the pork chef; he's Muslim and they consider eating pork sinful, and what's even worse is that the man hates to cook at all. It was like punishment to him and he didn't do anything at all wrong, not anything against company policy, anyway. Mr. Richardson assigning it to him was just wrong."

"Well, your first job is to assign someone who loves cooking pork and is proud of his cooking skills to write a pork program."

"That would be Dave Wilson, he really wanted that assignment and complained so noisily when he didn't get it that Richardson threatened to fire him. He complained even more than Mohamed did, even."

"Excellent, we'll need a barbecue program as well. Does Mister Wilson like cooking barbecue?"

Kowalski grinned. "He probably knows more about barbecue than any of us other engineers or programmers, and he's really good, even has his own recipe for sauce. He brought some in one day when we had a pot luck, and it was some of the best barbecue I've ever eaten. Mister Richardson has him programming robots to make coffee since you talked to him."

"He *does* drink coffee, doesn't he?"

"He practically lives on it, but he won't touch the coffee the robots are making now. He's kind of a coffee snob, we'll have great coffee when it's done."

"Will it take him long?"

"No, Dave hacks out code faster than anybody else here. Sometimes it's a little bloated, but programs can be trimmed down later, and every coffee drinker here, which is most of us, is sick of wasting their time making coffee when the robots should be able to. Knowing Dave, he'll have it done today or tomorrow."

The CEO said "I want you to do some reassignments. If anybody hates what they're designing or programming, give them something they like and are good at. Are any of your people less than competent?"

Kowalski grinned. "Not since you fired Mister Richardson."

"Who programmed the maids?"

"I'm not sure," Kowalski replied. "They were programmed before I started here. I think it was Mr. Richardson."

"They seem to have a bad habit of catching fire," the CEO remarked.

"I'm surprised they all don't catch fire more often, sir. Financial makes us buy the cheapest bot batteries on the market, making it really hard to design around them so they *won't* catch fire. We have to add safeties and extra insulation, and that makes them more expensive than using good batteries. On top of that they don't last very long, even when they don't catch fire."

"Well, Mister Kowalski, it looks like you're getting off to a very good start. As You might guess, your biggest headache is going to be financial. Everyone in that department thinks their MBAs and accounting degrees make them able to boss other departments around. From now on I want our robots to all have the highest quality batteries available. If financial gives you any trouble with that or anything else, don't hesitate to shoot Mister Osbourne or me an email."

"Yes sir. Thank you."

"I don't just have an MBA, Mr. Kowalski, I hold a Masters degree in electrical engineering myself as well, that's how we started this company. Mr. Osbourne has a mechanical engineering degree, and we bought two beat up old wrecks and made a better ship out of the two of them than anyone else's and then we grew from there. As an engineer I know that between cheap, fast, or good, you can have two if your teams are competent, but never all three. I expect our engineers to be top rate..."

"They are now, Mr. Green."

"Excellent. Now, I want good. Always, I want quality. When your engineers are designing, I want them to focus on that. We're spending way too much on repairs. Don't let financial talk you into cheap, we need quality. If the decision is between cheap and fast then let them decide unless it has to do with security or safety. Cost doesn't matter when it comes to safety or security. But never, ever skimp on quality for any reason."

"Yes sir, that's like a breath of fresh air. Nobody enjoys designing or programming crap."

"And you're going to be getting reports from boat captains, I want you to read them. You'll find them to be useful.

"I hope you and your engineers won't mind, but I'm splitting security into another division that will be headed by someone with military experience. Of course, they'll be working closely with your group. They can decide what weapons and defenses they need, and your shop can design and build them. Of course, if you have suggestions for them, tell them. And of course, cryptology will remain in the engineering department.

"Do you like pork, Mister Kowalski?"

"Not really. It's way too expensive, anyway."

"Well, if you did like it you could afford it once in a while now. Your new title comes with a new, much larger salary along with your new and harder duties. Oh, and speaking of pork we need to find a way to make up to Mister Nisbah for the horrible assignment Richardson gave him. Ask him what a Muslim needs but our boats don't have and if he'd like to design it."

"Yes, sir, I'd do that anyway."

"Okay, now lets go meet your staff."

"They're all waiting in conference room three," Kowalski said. "That's where I was when you called me, we were waiting for your visit."

After they entered the big conference room, the CEO said "Ladies and gentlemen, I have some good news for you all. I have appointed Mister Kowalski as your department head..."

The room burst into cheers and applause, making Green wait a minute to finish.

"I have some even better news than that," he said after the applause died down. "How many of you are working on projects Mister Richardson gave you that you hate? Those who are, please raise your hand."

A majority of them raised their hands.

"Well, Mister Kowalski is going to fix that. We're no longer going to have Hindus programming robots to cook beef and Muslims to program pork chefs. When the meeting is over, see Mister Kowalski for assignment changes, let him know what you would like to be working on and what you hate doing.

"Are there any questions? Any suggestions?"

Chapter Thirty One

Coffee

An alarm woke me up at quarter after six. What the hell? Fire in P117? I put on a robe, and as I trudged down there Tammy was running into the commons. I wondered what was going on.

I got to Passenger quarters one seventeen and it was a damned drill, the light was red but wasn't flashing and I didn't smell any smoke. I really didn't expect to, because except for Tammy's quarters none of the rest of the passenger section was occupied, all the apartments were locked, and wall panels blowing up is pretty rare, even on a new boat. Most fires are caused by old maids and on this trip, a stupid passenger. I don't know why they have those damned robots cleaning empty quarters.

I passed Tammy on the way back. "I missed Rilla," she said. "I forgot she got up early to eat."

As I passed the commons on the way home I saw the obese blonde German woman leaning back in a chair, an empty plate with the remains of breakfast on it in front of her and an eyedropper on the floor next to her. I was glad I read Tammy's book, the German woman was going to want a dildo in a minute or two and I sure didn't want it to be me. I hurried back to my quarters and started coffee, since it was too late to go back to sleep, and headed to the head to pee.

Zero G football was in the semifinals and I caught the last quarter of the game. Belgium beat Brazil two to one. I told the robot to make scrambled eggs, toast, and hash browns and went to shit and shower.

God DAMN that Mexican food, my asshole was on fire! It felt like I was shitting flames. Why do I keep forgetting what spicy food does to my asshole? Fuck!

When I got out of the shower Destiny was at the table wearing a robe and drinking coffee. "G'mornin' sunshine," she said. "You're sure up early."

"Yeah, I had an alarm. Just a drill, though. What time is it?"

"I don't know."

"Computer, what damned... no, scratch that. I mean 'disregard'. Computer, what time is it on board the ship?"

"The present time is seven twelve."

I decided to set up a holographic map of EMF in my living room, even though it should be quite a while before we saw any pirates. I didn't know it then but they would show up early. Way too early.

Destiny had the news on the video. Some scandal in the capitol but I wasn't paying attention; I still hadn't had enough coffee.

At five 'til eight I went to the pilot room. Everything checked out, so before I started my inspection I set another holomap up in there as well.

The maps marked spacemarks and radio transmissions and used what engineers called a "passive radar system" to mark objects, but I really don't know what that means. I thought again "I'm taking some classes when I reach Mars."

I went to inspect downstairs, but as I passed the commons it was empty and I smelled smoke. It was one of the waiters that was smoking, so I pulled out my fone. "Computer, shut R47 down and send a repair robot."

I went outside and called the computer again, instructing it to seal the commons and depressurize it until R47 was powered down and taken in for repairs.

The heavy German woman walked up looking angry. "Hey, Joe," she said with her heavy German accent, "I'm hungry, why is the restaurant closed?" Christ, she was in there eating and dropping not too long earlier when there was the stupid drill in the passenger section.

The passenger section had quarters like apartments with their own cooking and serving and coffee robots, but cargo pens are single rooms with a sink and toilet, although of course there's also furniture in them when we're carrying human cargo. People flying in the cargo section have to eat in the commons, or have robots bring their meals from there.

"One of the robots is smoking so there's no air in there right now. It won't be long before you can eat," I said.

"But I'm starved!" she exclaimed, her accent even thicker than usual. Christ, how much food was enough for this woman?

Tammy walked up. "Hi, John, Rilla, what's going on?"

"Smoking robot," I said. "Shouldn't take more than ten minutes."

"Ten minutes!" the always hungry blonde said. "I'll die of starvation!"

Tammy said "I'll take care of it, John." Right then a robot wheeled up and the commons door opened. Tammy and the fat girl went inside as a robot dragged the burned up other robot out and towed it to the maintenance shop.

I finished heading for the stairs. Damned stairs.

The working generator was okay, so I inspected engines. The ones I had shut down were first. Number sixty three was fine so I started it back up and noted it in the log. Next was twenty four, and it checked out okay so I restarted it as well. Even number seventeen was good so I started it back up, too. If I could add two and two and get something close to four I'd probably left it shut down, but I ain't psychic. All of the rest of the engines were fine; all engines were online.

The broken generator was still broken, of course. But everything else was in great shape for once. I trudged back up the stairs.

The only one in the commons was Lek, the only one of the three Thais on board who could talk English okay. She was wearing jeans and a t-shirt and sipping coffee. A dropper with coffee? According to Tammy's book that shouldn't happen. I called Tammy and gave her the news.

"Really? Wow," she said. "I'll be right there."

Lek said "Hello, Captain."

I said hello as Tammy came in carrying a pot of coffee and sat down with Lek. "Here, Lek," she said, "I brought some good coffee. But should you be drinking coffee at all?"

"Animals no drink coffee," Lek said, "and I no want be animal. I not remember what coffee supposed to taste like."

I left her to Tammy, she was the expert, after all, and I went home.

"You're later than usual," Destiny said.

"Busy morning. Smoking robot, hungry fat girl, started a couple of engines..."

"Okay, okay," she said laughing. "Lets have lunch. T-bone and mashed potatoes and slaw okay?"

"Sure," I said, and had the robot bring me a glass of shike.

After we ate we took a short walk then watched some old two dimensional movie about the American Civil War, even though the actual war part only took a couple of minutes at the very first part of the movie. I think it was called "Lincoln".

By the time it was over it was supper time. We had stew, watched one of the movies Destiny called a "spaghetti western", watched an episode of *Rawhide* and listened to some Hendrix for a while before we went to bed.

Chapter Thirty Two

Engine

An alarm woke me up at quarter to seven, and for once I didn't mind a bit. In fact, I was really glad it woke me up because I was in the middle of a *really* weird dream. A herd of cows was stampeding towards me, only they were running on their hind legs, wearing cowboy hats, and somehow carrying big butcher knives in their front hooves, all singing Hendrix's *I Don't Live Today* while coming at me. Too many westerns and too much twentieth century music, I guess.

It was engine seventeen, something was wrong with it. I shut it down from the pilot room and started a pot of coffee perking before I shit, showered, and shaved. Destiny woke up about the time I was getting dressed.

"What time is it?" she asked.

"I don't know, maybe ten or fifteen after seven."

"You're up early again!"

"Yeah," I said. "Alarm woke me up from a really weird dream, there's something wrong with engine seventeen. I shut it down and corrected course so eight o'clock should be easy this morning. Hungry?"

"I probably will be. What are you having?"

"Steak and scrambled eggs and toast. Should I have the robot make you that?"

"Sure, only I want my eggs sunny side up. Is there any good coffee made?"

"Yeah, I made a pot, most of it is still left."

She got out of bed and put on a robe and followed me into the dining room, where the robot was already cooking our breakfast. I put the news on. Not much new, some problem at that big Venus station, an outbreak of some disease they thought had been eradicated decades earlier. They were worried it might get back to Earth.

I think they only have the news to scare people and make them worry.

We ate our breakfast and drank coffee and Destiny started a second pot as I went back to the pilot room for the eight o'clock readings. Like I figured, they were fine. I was sure glad because this was going to be another busy day, what with number seventeen shut down and today I had to inspect cargo.

The passenger section was, like usual, a big waste of time. Cargo were all asleep except the German woman, who was in the commons with Tammy, and a girl named Angel, who was in her quarters bending over the sink. She turned around and looked at me with those scary red monster eyes and I freaked out and ran, and ordered the door locked behind me and called Tammy.

"We have a serious problem," I said. "Angel is going through withdrawal."

"What? I left her a dose, someone must have stolen it. I'll be right there." She came running down the hall holding her fone and a bottle of drops. "How bad is she?"

"Bad," I said. "Redeye bad. That Angel girl was the scariest thing I've ever seen in my life."

"Oh, no," she said. "I'll be right back, try to keep that door closed. If she gets out we're all dead."

"Wait! Where are you going?"

"To rig up a spray bottle. This is going to be very dangerous but it has to be done." She ran to her quarters.

I had an idea that might not be so dangerous and pulled out my fone. "Computer," I said, "what's the best way to knock that bitch out?"

The fone said "Parse error, there are no female dogs on board and 'knock' is not in context. Please rephrase."

Who programs these God damned stupid things,

anyway? Back when computers were new, science fiction movies had computers that could think. These stupid computers sure can't. God damn it, I was going to have to talk like I went to college... only I ain't went to college, damn it.

"Uh, how can I..." I had to think a minute. "Uh, make the woman in cargo twenty two go to sleep fast with the least amount of harm?"

The fone said, in writing of course, "waiting until she falls asleep naturally would cause the least harm." Stupid computer. Damn it, I said fast!

"What will cause her to, uh... lose consciousness *quickly* with the least amount of harm, as quickly as possible?"

"Replacing the air with an inert gas would accomplish the task," it said. Whatever the hell an "inert gas" is.

"Okay," I told it, "replace the air in cargo twenty two with an inert gas."

"Please choose which inert gas you wish to replace it with."

God damn computers! "What gas will knock... uh, put her to sleep, uh, make her unconscious with the least damage?"

"Nitrogen, he..."

"Computer, replace the air in cargo twenty two with nitrogen and then open the door when she goes to sleep... uh, becomes unconscious."

"Complying."

Tammy came running back carrying a spray bottle just as the door was opening. "It's okay," I said. "She's not conscious, I knocked her out." Angel was laying right by the door.

"Wow, John, remind me not to piss *you* off," she said. She took care of Angel while I finished my inspection. There was some minor damage to her sink, and I wondered what the hell that crazy animal was trying to do. As I was leaving the room, a medic Tammy had summoned rolled in.

I'd do the commons and sick bay after the engines and generators.

Everything was fine down there, all things considered. The generator was a little warm, but readings said it had been a lot warmer at seven.

All the engines except seventeen were fine. Seventeen had shorted out; we were lucky the alarm went off or either the generator would have probably been damaged so bad that it would have to be rebuilt, or the rest of the engines might have fried, or both. I logged it; the robot was already working on it. We'd be fine with only one engine out. At one time earlier in the trip I'd had three or four that weren't lit, but there are a hell of a lot of the huge things.

I checked out the rest of the monstrously big engines. That's where I spend most of my work day usually, downstairs inspecting thrusters since there were so many of them and they all had control panels and readouts that had to be inspected and logged.

I trudged back up the five damned flights of stairs and decided to have lunch before finishing inspections; it was already twelve thirty and I was starved.

I had a cheeseburger and Afghan style fried potatoes for lunch. Destiny had a steak chef salad, joking about pork. Her pig jokes made me think about the German woman.

"I still have a little more work," I told her. "Engines took forever today because of number seventeen, I spent over half an hour on just that one alone. I still have to inspect the sick bay and commons. Want to go for a walk when we finish eating?"

"Sure," she said. "I'll come along."

We finished eating and walked to sick bay. I inspected it and we went into the commons, where Lek and Tammy were drinking coffee and eating turkey sandwiches. Lek was still wearing clothes and acting pretty damned ladylike for a drug addict. Tammy was doing some damned good work with that one, she should be proud. Lek should be proud, too.

We got back home at two or three and destiny put on an old two dimensional comedy western named "Wagons East". It was a really silly movie and we laughed our asses off watching it. Destiny said that part of this one had to be done in a computer because one of the stars, the fat guy who played the wagon master, died before they finished shooting and they had to map his face to a body double. She said computers used in movies was still really new when that one was made.

When it was over we ate a poor man's dinner; prime rib, baked potato, salad, and wine. I only drank one glass, I hate hangovers. Especially wine hangovers.

I did have two beers while we watched *The Underpass*. That's a new one, you guys probably saw it already.

We listened to some old classical blues and cuddled when it was over and then we went to bed.

Chapter Thirty Three

Smiles

Destiny woke me up about seven thirty; I'd been the one up early the day before because of that engine. "Wake up, sleepyhead, or you won't have time for breakfast," she said. She'd already made coffee and had the robots make chicken cheese omelettes.

God but I love that woman, meeting her was the best thing that ever happened to me in my life. Of course, were it not for the monsters I'd probably never have met her. You take the wonderful with the insanely horrible, I guess.

"That stupid computer," she said. "I wanted a turkey cheese omelette and the dumb thing kept telling me that there were no Turkish cheeses on the menu. I finally gave up, so it's chicken."

"We'll have them tomorrow," I said. "You have to tell it cheese and turkey."

We watched the news while we ate, but like always there was nothing new. A war had broken out in Africa, but there's always a war somewhere, it seems. People are stupid.

Lankham Farms in Mexico closed down, citing Mexico's new environmental laws. The environmental regulations in almost all countries were strict to the point that raising pork just wasn't economical enough to earn any money. Since Lankham closed there were only a few African countries that still produced pork. About the only place you could buy pork was from the fanciest farm restaurants where they grew the food and raised the animals they cooked and served, using human cooks and wait staff, the kind you had to be a Dewey

Green to afford eating at. They only raised a few hogs at a time because of the environmental laws.

Like I care about the price of pork. Sheesh.

I finished breakfast, showered and got dressed, kissed Destiny and went to the pilot room for my normal morning routine.

Everything in the pilot room checked out. There were no upstairs inspections today so I trudged down the five damned flights of stairs, which is better than trudging up them, and inspected the generators and engines. Yep, port generator and engine seventeen still broke. A robot was still working on seventeen so I logged it.

I got done quick today! Probably wasn't even noon yet. Destiny was in the commons drinking coffee with Tammy and Lek, who was still wearing clothes, although different ones. I wondered where she got them, probably traded drops to the naked animals for theirs. Or maybe Tammy gave her some, I don't know. I sat down with them and complimented Lek.

"Thank you," she said.

"You've come a long way, Lek. You should be proud."

She smiled widely. Thailand is known as "the Land of Smiles" and unless they were short of drops the three on board were smiling almost every time I saw them. Lots different than that German woman, who was always frowning and never seemed to smile. It had been quite a while since Lek's pupils were different sizes, although they were usually at least a little bloodshot.

"Doctor Winters help me," she said. I was startled. "Tammy?" I said, really confused.

"She's smart, John. She figured me out after a couple of weeks and confronted me. She noticed that I was the only one wearing clothes and that I had plenty of drops, and she guessed correctly that I was pretending to be an addicted prostitute and asked me why I was faking it, so I admitted that I was really a scientist studying them and trying to find a cure, and asked her to keep it secret."

"I no tell anybody," Lek said. "I only call her doctor when we alone. She say I not animal because I have good manners and respect, and animals no have manners or respect. I would have figured out sooner except her eyes."

Tammy laughed. "I used phenylephrine. It's a harmless medication that ophthalmologists have used to dilate patients' eyes for examination for centuries. A drop in one eye made me look like I was on angel tears. It fooled everyone but Lek."

I asked "What was up with that one woman yesterday?"

"She knocked her drops off of the sink and thought they went down the drain. She went through withdrawal for nothing, if she'd been in her right mind she would have realized that there's no way that bottle would fit down that drain."

"Do they always go through withdrawal that bad, that fast?" I asked.

"No," she said. "She had to have been out of them for at least a couple of days. Maybe she lost them like she did yesterday, or maybe someone stole them. It's something I worry about constantly."

Then she started talking Thai with Lek. Lek said "We need speak English, they no understand." I gathered that Tammy spoke very good Thai and communication was easier between them in that language.

"Uh," I said, "Are you working right now, Tammy?"

"Well, kind of," she said.

"I'm sorry, we're in the way" I responded.

Destiny blushed. "Oh, God, Tammy, I'm sorry! You're making great progress, though. Both of you. Come on, John."

We went home, ate lunch, and Destiny put on a two dimensional science fiction movie from the twentieth century, and it was funny as hell. I think it was called "Star Wars" or something. I'm still chuckling over "these are not the droids you're looking for." Those old movies were a lot funnier than the ones they make today.

Huh? I don't know, I think it was Italian food, Destiny ordered it. Some kind of cheesy noodles with meat and tomato sauce.

Huh? Oh, there's quite a few of those *Star Wars* movies. After the first one was so successful they made it into a trilogy. Back then computers were still way too primitive to make movies in so it was all models and puppets and probably drawings by hand. Oddly they shot episodes four through six first, and didn't shoot one through three for another twenty years, probably because the technology to do it wasn't there. It was another fifteen years before another one was made after the first six.

Then we had beef and beans for supper and watched *Forever Old*, a new holo.

We listened to the Vaughn brothers for a while and went to bed.

Chapter Thirty Four

Drills

I got woke up early again, about five thirty this time. Fire in passengers quarters number forty seven. God damned drills, but I had to get up and inspect forty seven anyway. I put on a robe and trudged down there.

Yep, just a stupid drill. I noticed that Tammy was in the commons with the German woman as I walked past on my way back home. It was still early enough that I could still get another hour's sleep or so.

Nope, as soon as I got back there another damned alarm went off, this time a fire in engine seventeen. This one might be real, so I hurried down there and told the computer to deliver some nasty robot coffee.

The computer wouldn't let me in at first, it must have been in a vacuum. The door finally opened, and the robot that had been working on it was charred and still smoking a little. I unhooked it from the engine, and another one rolled up for me to hook up, and a third dragged the smoking robot to the repair shop.

I logged it and trudged back up the five damned flights of stairs towards home, but by then it was too late to go back to bed, quarter after six. I made a pot of real coffee and put a game on, but it was almost over. When it was over I switched it to the always old news.

Nothing new, of course, they were still trying to scare people about the Venus virus. Destiny came in, kissed me, and poured a cup of coffee. "You're up early again," she said.

"Yeah," I replied, "fire drill in the passenger section

and a burned up robot down in the engine room. I was up at five thirty. I'm sure glad we went to bed early!"

"Did you eat yet?"

"No, you hungry?"

"Yeah. Computer, make a cheese and turkey omelette."

It replied "affirmative," of course. I said "Computer, a turkey Denver."

The stupid thing said "Error, no Turkish dishes named Denver are listed in the database."

God damned stupid computer. "A Denver omelette with turkey meat you dumb computer."

"There is no meat from that country."

I sighed. Destiny giggled. "A Denver omelette with bird meat," I said.

"Please name the bird."

"Turkey."

"Affirmative."

"Fuck you."

Destiny laughed. "Had your shower yet?"

"No," I said, "Want to take one together?"

"Sure," she said, with a twinkle in her eye. God, but I love that woman.

We had a pretty long, really fun shower and ate our breakfast. By then it was almost eight, so I kissed her and took a cup of coffee to the pilot room. We were going the right way and all the computers were agreeing with each other that everything was cool.

After that I had inspection. The German woman was eating in the commons and the rest were asleep, except Lek, who was in her quarters reading, still dressed. I complimented her on her clothing.

"Thank you," she said. "I want Doctor Winters to cure me."

"So do I," I said. "I want her to cure all of you."

"I want that too," she said.

I went down those five damned flights of stairs again to

157

the bottom of the boat. The good generator was still good and the busted generator was still busted. So was engine seventeen, with the robot I'd plugged into it still working on it.

It had been an easy inspection. I made my long trek back up all those God damned stairs. There were fifty or so women in the commons, pretty much behaving themselves.

As I went in my quarters Destiny said "You're a little early. Done?"

"Yeah, I hope so. Are you hungry?"

She said yes, and laughed. "Computer, ham and beans."

The computer replied, of course, "There are no pork products on the menu."

I laughed, and said "I wonder if there's a kind of bean named a 'Hammond Bean'? I'll bet the robot couldn't serve them even if they were listed in the database! I think I'll have prime rib, baked potato and a glass of wine."

"Sounds good to me," Destiny said.

Right then a light lit up on the map. "Damn it," I said, and went to the pilot room to listen in. Thankfully it wasn't pirates, it was just a boat from a different shipping company about five light minutes away.

The robot was finished cooking lunch right after I got back, so we ate. Then we watched an old two dimensional movie called "The Blues Brothers", and I loved that movie! Funny as hell and it had some really great old classical music. Some of the musical greats from the time, like Ray Charles and John Lee Hooker and Aretha Franklin, were in it.

The closing credits were rolling on the screen when an alarm went off in cargo nine. I hoped it was a drill. "Is cargo nine occupied?" I asked the computer.

"Negative."

That was Lek's room; she was in the commons. The light on her door was solid red, so I went in to investigate; there was no fire.

I went to the commons to talk to Lek. "Here because of the fire drill?" I asked.

"Drill? I thought my apartment really on fire! Scared me when the alarm go off."

"Yeah, it was just a drill, you can go home if you want."

"Thank you, Captain," she said.

I went home myself and we had Polish sausage and sauerkraut with shikes for dinner. Destiny put on an old two dimensional western, *True Grit*. She said that there were two of them and each of the movies were better than the book, which she'd read and said "wasn't very well written".

We'd each had a glass of wine with lunch and finished the bottle watching the western, since it would be sour by the next morning if we didn't. No sense in wasting it.

We listened to a little Clapton when the movie was over and then we went to bed. It was still early but Destiny had gotten up earlier than normal and I'd gotten up way early, and I was just plumb wore out.

Chapter Thirty Five

Couch

I woke up about twenty after seven. I put on a robe and trudged bleary-eyed to the kitchen to start a pot of coffee, and Destiny woke up just as I was going to the head. I still think that's a stupid name for a bathroom.

She had the robot make French toast and sausage and was in the living room drinking coffee and watching the news when I went in there after I got dressed. "I wish we had some pork sausage," she said.

"You should have brought some," I replied. "I wish we were on Mars!"

"Yeah, I should have," she said. "Oh, well, I ought to be able to get it on Mars when we get there."

"It's four times as expensive there," I said. "Shipping costs, you know."

She smiled. "That's okay, I can afford it even if it does make me feel guilty."

"Why does it make you feel guilty? I could see it if you were spending the rent money on pork."

"I don't know," she said. "I'm just frugal by nature. I hate spending money even though I'll never run out. Maybe I'm just crazy."

Huh? I don't know, we were gabbing and not paying attention to the stupid news. We ate our breakfast in the living room, and the map lit up just as I was finishing eating. I went to the pilot room, mug in hand. It was about ten 'til so I'd be in there a while.

The blip was a cargo ship from another shipping company. I wondered why other companies didn't have radar absorbing coatings and passive radar and all that other stealthy stuff like ours did. Our boats are easy to hide and hard to find unless we want to be found. Good thing, too, or Bill's goose would have been cooked when he ran across the pirates I rained on, and they would have had his boat.

Eight o'clock finally came. Funny how long it takes ten minutes to pass when you have absolutely nothing at all to do. It looked like this was going to be a really easy day; no course corrections and the only red light was engine seventeen, and I didn't have to inspect upstairs today.

I stopped by our quarters... yeah, our quarters, she was living with me and we're getting married. So shut the fuck up before I walk out of here, asshole. Anyway, I stopped by our quarters to fill my cup, kissed Destiny, and started my trek to my dungeon, with its torture equipment. Huh? The stairs, of course. I hate those God damned stairs.

The German woman was, as usual, in the commons eating. Tammy walked past and said "hi".

I went down the torture equipment, which isn't as bad as coming up it, to inspect my dungeon.

Everything checked out, all the lights were green and all the readings were normal and the only robot doing anything was on number seventeen. I hauled my aching back up the torturous stairs.

The commons was just starting to fill with droppers and was still pretty empty. I must not have spent much time at all downstairs. Destiny wasn't home, probably in Tammy's quarters, I thought. "What time is it?" I asked the computer. Wow, only eleven! I was home really early today.

I turned on the video and checked listings on my tablet. All right! A zero gravity football game was just starting so I switched it to that.

About five after, Destiny came home. "Wow!" she said. "You're home really early today!"

"Yeah," I said. "I haven't had a day this light since the

first week we were in space. Cross your fingers! Want to watch this game with me, or do you want to do something else?"

"I like football," she said. "We'll watch the game." Right then the map lit, but only for a second.

"I'll be right back," I said. I went to the pilot room to see what the light was, but it hadn't been a good enough signal to even tell what kind of vessel it was. I went back home. A robot was cooking hot dogs and french fries and making potato salad.

Huh? How the hell should I know what the damned hot dogs were made of, except I know it wasn't pork.

I missed a goal while I was checking out the blip, St. Louis had scored against Novosibirsk. One nothing, and it was really early in the game.

We moved to the dining room when lunch was done cooking and turned the game on in there. By the time we got the video turned on and on the right channel, it was one up; Novosibirsk had scored. Wow, two goals this fast?

Destiny said there used to be a very violent game called "American Football" but it eventually died out because so many of its players got dementia from head injuries. Weird.

The cook wheeled over with our lunch. When we finished eating we moved back into the living room. Two to one Novosibirsk. Damn, I'd missed all three goals.

When the game ended it was still two to one. Novosibirsk had beaten St. Louis. St. Louis had two great baseball teams, one Earth and one zero gravity, but their football teams both really sucked. They were almost as bad as Chicago's and Paris' teams, two cities that seem to lose at every sport they play.

We watched some old short gray movies; two episodes of *Rawhide*, part of a silly serial called "Buck Rogers," a different *Untouchables* movie that wasn't nearly as good as the long one that had colors in it that we'd watched quite a while ago, and one with colors called "Emergency!" about a fire department and hospital in the second half of the twentieth century.

Destiny asked "How about burritos for supper?"

"No way in hell," I said. "If I eat Mexican food my asshole is on fire the next day!" She had a burrito and I had beef stew.

She put on *Hardly Ever After*, a new holo. I fell asleep on the couch, and she woke me up when it was really bedtime. You would think I'd have stayed awake after such an easy day.

Chapter Thirty Six

Heat

It was only a little after seven when I woke up. Destiny was asleep, so I put on a robe, started coffee, and went to the head to take a piss. I turned on the video; nothing on but the news. Nothing new, some "special report" about Martian piracy. Of course, they didn't say anything I didn't already know. I finished my cup and took a shower. Destiny was waking up as I was getting dressed.

"You're up early again! Another alarm, sweetheart?"

"No," I said, "I just woke up early. I don't know why I fell asleep so early last night. It isn't like yesterday was a busy day or anything. Hungry?"

"I don't know, what time is it?"

I had to ask the stupid talking table. It said seventeen after seven. She got a cup of coffee and told the computer to make a turkey omelette, and again the stupid damned thing said "There are no Turkish omelette dishes listed in the database."

Stupid computer. She sighed. "Stupid computer," she said, "I want an omelette with turkey meat. A turkey omelette has nothing to do with the country called Turkey."

The idiotic thing replied "Parse error, please rephrase."

"God!" Destiny exclaimed, "Jesus but Dad's computers are stupid. Computer!"

"Waiting for input."

"I want an omelette with turkey meat."

"There is no meat that has come from that country."

"Turkey the bird, damn it!"

"Parse error, please rephrase."

"What meats are available for omelettes?"

"Chicken, duck, turkey, and beef."

"An omelette with turkey meat."

"There is no meat from that country," the idiotic thing repeated.

She was becoming annoyed. "Damn it, computer, I want an omelette with bird meat."

"Please name the bird."

"Turkey."

"Acknowledged."

"That must the dumbest computer I ever saw," she said.

"Waiting for input," the computer stupidly said, obviously picking up on the word "computer".

"Damn it," she started.

"Roast beef and cheese omelette," I said.

"Complying."

By the time breakfast was finished cooking I only had fifteen minutes to eat, the stupid computer had wasted most of our morning time together because its programming was so idiotic.

The "special report" about pirates was still on when I left for work, and still didn't have anything to say that I didn't already know. The news is almost as stupid as the stupid computer.

I left for the pilot room with two minutes to spare. I hadn't even finished my breakfast. God damned computer!

There was a light on the map as I went into the pilot room. Damn, but that computer has shitty timing; I had to do readings and couldn't check it out.

Luckily everything was normal; the computers were agreeing, we were on course, and it showed nothing except engine seventeen and the port generator had anything wrong with them.

The light was pirates, about four and a half light minutes away, but they weren't headed anywhere near us. A few minutes later it was off the radar.

Still, it was worrying. Even though we had tangled with pirates farther out, this was the first trip I'd ever run that I'd seen pirates anywhere near this far from Mars. And it would still be well over a week before we met the fleet.

I went back to our quarters to fill my coffee. Destiny asked "Trouble?"

"Pirates," I said. "They showed up at the fringe of radar but are gone now. Remember, you can't talk about pirates to anybody."

"I know, don't worry."

The robots hadn't thrown the rest of my breakfast away, so I finished eating before starting inspections, chatting about droppers and pirates with Destiny. I kissed her and started inspections. Luckily I only had to inspect downstairs. Luckily? Hell, there were all those damned stairs... but I guess that has nothing to do with luck.

At the bottom of the stairs I started with the generator, and there was nothing wrong with anything except number sixty two, which had a robot attached, and seventeen. I logged sixty two and started towards all those damned steps.

But as I passed the starboard generator, there was a yellow light. What the hell? It was fine when I went down there. I looked closer and checked the panel – it was dangerously warm. Damn it, that should set an alarm off! Looking closer, number seventeen was drawing an obscene amount of power. I hit the generator's emergency shutoff, and the readings said the batteries were draining at a rapid rate as gravity got lighter.

I took off at a run to seventeen, and the robot attached to it was starting to smoke badly. I also saw that the robot had plugged itself into the main power. I tried to disconnect it from the engine, but the lead was too hot to touch. My fingers were going to be blistered. I kicked the robot's main power cable loose from mains with my boot as the robot burst into flames and the alarm went off. I got the hell out of there and ran back to the generator room.

The batteries weren't draining like they were; something in the robot had shorted and had been feeding number seventeen with the mains it had plugged itself into. At least the yellow light had gone out, but it was still way too hot for my liking, it being our only remaining generator. I'd let it cool some more before I fired it back up.

I went back to seventeen, which was in a vacuum by now. I waited for the door to open. Still smoking, the robot was half melted. This robot wouldn't be doing any more repairs! It was surely totaled. I found a pair of gloves and was able to disconnect it. I got some cable cutters, cut off the plug and plugged it back into the engine's robot plug. Maybe other robots couldn't try to fix it like that. I hoped so, anyway.

I walked back to the generator. It had cooled almost to normal, so I restarted it. Gravity started to rise again.

My fone buzzed; it was Destiny. "What's going on, John?"

"Trouble with an engine and the generator," I said. "I hope it didn't upset the droppers too much. I'm on my way upstairs now, have you had lunch yet?

"Well, yeah, it's two in the afternoon. I was worried."

"So was I," I said, "but I think it's okay now. Have the robot make me a sandwich, would you?" I was starved, but I'd been too busy to even notice I'd been hungry.

I trudged wearily up all those stairs to correct the ship's course. Destiny brought my lunch to the pilot room. "You're sweet," I said, "thanks, but this will only take a few minutes and I'm done... I hope. Just put it on the table and I'll be right there." She kissed me and left.

I went and finished my lunch, and had a beer with it. This had really been a crappy day. Shit, except for Destiny the whole damned trip was a trip through hell.

We sat on the couch cuddling and I didn't even hardly notice that an old gray Dracula movie was on. I must have been really tired, because even though the movie didn't have any colors, Dracula's eyes looked red.

Destiny was comforting me after my bad day, and I fell asleep in her arms. She woke me up and led me to bed, but I was too tired to do anything but sleep.

Chapter Thirty Seven

Arena

I woke up about seven, maybe a little earlier. I laid there a while before I got up and started coffee.

I did my business in the head, and Destiny was just getting up. We had eggs over easy, sausage, and toast while watching the "news". It was hard to hold the fork; I had blisters on my fingers from the plug on that stupid damned robot.

They were trying to worry people even more about the Venus virus; someone had died. One of our competitors had a fire in its factory in Peru and somebody died in that, too.

Someone tried to assassinate Britain's Prime Minister and their bobbies put seventy three bullets in the would-be assassin, as well as a few more bullets in some innocent bystanders for good measure. Why in the hell can't cops shoot straight?

I was hoping today would be a lot lighter than yesterday. At least all I had to inspect was downstairs. The eight o'clock readings were normal, so I sauntered down the hall to the damned stairs. Lek and Tammy were in the commons drinking coffee and reading. I marveled at the job Tammy was doing with Lek, Lek was really coming along.

As I walked past I heard Tammy telling Lek "Your eyes are really getting bloodshot. Better have a dose before you start hurting and I can't help you." I didn't hear what was said after, I was just passing by.

Two droppers were arguing in the hallway so I called Tammy, and she said she'd take care of it.

Down my damned stairs everything was okay, except

another robot was trying to plug itself in to seventeen, but was too stupid to know it had to unplug the plug I'd cut from the burned up robot. I logged it and trekked back up those damned stairs.

Tammy had to spray one of the two I'd called her about, and the other one was being treated in sick bay for two black eyes and a concussion. Luckily, Tammy hadn't been injured. Destiny and her was just coming out of the commons as I passed. "Rough one," Tammy said. "I'm sure glad my bottle worked!"

"How did it happen?" I asked.

"The one in sick bay had stolen her drops two days in a row. The one I sprayed was almost redyed by the time I got the spray bottle and got all the way here. Quite frightening, but it turned out all right. Maybe Karen will think twice about stealing drops from now on after that, but I really doubt it."

"Those poor women," Destiny said.

"No kidding," I replied. "I wonder what time it is?"

"I don't know," she said, "but my stomach says it's lunch time. Want to have lunch with us, Tammy?"

"Sorry, I can't. I have a paper to work on and don't have time to eat right now. I need to document the bottle's effectiveness and want to get a passage or two written down before I forget what I was going to write."

We went home and had fritter dogs and Turkish potatoes. I'll bet there's no way at all to tell that God damned stupid computer to make roast turkey and Turkish spuds.

We had the news on as we ate. The closing of the Mexican hog farm, a huge operation that used a lot of human labor, caused a ripple effect through the Mexican economy and its two biggest banks went bankrupt. The closing of the banks had caused riots and Mexico had to get help from the American military. There was talk of Mexico becoming part of the United states. Most Mexicans wanted it, but few Americans did because of fears of what it would do to their economy.

Destiny put on a short, really stupid twentieth century

two dimensional science fiction movie, *Arena,* about a space-ship's captain who has to fight a giant sentient lizard with a really bad costume. It was so stupid it was almost funny. Traveling faster than light was dumb enough, but the rest of the show was even dumber. No robots and everything looked really primitive, especially the costume the actor playing the lizard was wearing.

We watched another *Emergency*; that one was pretty good. Then a short western, I forgot what it was called but it was a gray movie about a nineteenth century rancher and his young son.

We ate some Irish sandwich Destiny said was an ancient Irish working man's lunch for dinner, with French fries and cole slaw, and she put on a modern holo named "Yesterday's Promise". Then we cuddled to some old classical blues and went to bed.

Chapter Thirty Eight

Sneakers

I woke up a little early, maybe ten or fifteen minutes after seven. I started coffee and did my morning bathroom... oh, shut up. Head, bathroom, what difference does it make? "Head" is a dumb name for a room you take a bath in, anyway, almost as stupid as bow, stern, port, and starboard. At least those make sense in an ocean ship even though they don't on a space ship. "Head" don't even make sense in an ocean boat. What? Well, that's a good reason they started calling them that but even ocean boats weren't like that was for at least the last five hundred years back. So shut up before I walk out of here and they fire both of you.

Anyway, I was in the dining room drinking coffee and watching a zero gravity baseball game... What? You never watched zero G baseball? It's kind of like zero gravity golf except there's more to baseball; it has teams throwing and catching a ball that's bigger than a golf ball while people "run"... I guess that's what you'd call it, even though they were flying, from one pole to the next and golf is one on one and you just hit the ball into a hole. The sticks are similar, a zero gravity golf club isn't anything like an Earth-side golf club. Baseball bats are really similar to ground-side bats, though.

I can't believe you guys never watched zero G baseball or golf. I like them almost as much as zero G football. Anyway, when I was watching the game, Destiny came in the dining room wearing a robe. "What are you watching?" she asked.

"Zero gravity baseball, St. Louis against Chicago. Six to two Chicago's favor, they're in the bottom of the ninth and the bases are loaded. If McMurtrey doesn't get on base the game's over, and probably will be anyway unless he hits a home run, and home runs are really rare in zero G. If he does hit a homer I'll miss the end of the game because I have to go to work at eight." Of course, if he'd hit a single the game would still be in play unless they threw anybody else out...

She poured a cup of coffee and McMurtrey struck out. I switched it to the news and we had corned beef and cheese omelettes for breakfast. The epidemic on the Venus station was worse and three people had died from it. It was completely quarantined and supply ships couldn't even dock, they had to leave supplies floating in space and somebody from the station or maybe a robot, I don't know, the news didn't say, somehow they had to get them in the space station.

At eight I went to the pilot room to do my eight o'clock chores. It turned out to be a light morning, the computers were all agreeing and we didn't need a course correction. All the droppers were asleep except the German girl, who was in the commons eating. The generators were fine, except that one of the two wouldn't work. All the engines were fine except seventeen, which wasn't going to be lit before the Mars overhaul, since it destroyed two mechs and damned near ruined the last generator. The stupid robot was still trying to plug itself into seventeen. There weren't even any robots working on any of the other ones.

We had an early lunch, ham sandwiches and... yeah, I was just checking to see if you guys were paying attention, we really had Italian roast beef sandwiches and chips, and Destiny put a movie on.

We was watching the movie when I saw a light on the holographic map again. Huh? An old twentieth century western, *Rawhide* I think. Short movie, maybe forty minutes or so. It was in two dimensions, like I already said there wasn't no hologram movies back then. Hell, they didn't even have lasers and holograms need lasers. Haven't you guys been paying attention? I mentioned that show a bunch of times already.

173

This one didn't even have colors, just shades of gray. Weird. A lot of old movies were like that, I mentioned them before, too. Why? What difference does it make?

The map was a holo of nearby... huh? Maybe five or six light minutes. Come on, guys, it's standard, haven't you ever been on one of these boats? Anyway, it was a holo of any bodies close by and any EMF sources, didn't I say that earlier? ...and one lit up; it was another radio transmission. I hoped it was just another shipping company like the ones that had shown up earlier. The computer would record it, so I had Destiny pause the movie while I saw what the EMF was, and listened in.

Shit, pirate traffic! More pirates this far out? I sure didn't expect that! We were two weeks from Mars and the company fleet wouldn't be accompanying us for another week, which was twice as far as pirates normally went. I didn't expect anything but false alarms until we were almost to the fleet.

I stuck my head in the door of our quarters. "Sorry, hon, gotta work," I said.

"Is this movie boring you?"

"No, keep it paused until I get back. Look, hon, I have to go, there's pirates. This is serious and I have work to do. Remember, you can't mention pirates to anyone." I kissed her and went into the pilot room and looked at the holos there.

For once I caught a break, but unfortunately at some other boat captain's expense. It wasn't our company, I don't remember what company, I didn't really care. Anyway, the pirates thought he was me and started chasing him.

I masered Bill, hoping he was close enough that the signal would be strong enough to be understood. "Wild Bill, John here. Pirates ahead, go around if you have enough batteries. They think some other company's ship is me. I'm slowing down until they engage, then I'm hauling ass."

I addressed the women. "Ladies, it would be a really good idea to strap in right now because gravity might get weird." By now they knew what I meant when I said gravity was going to get weird. Unless they were short on drops and they probably wouldn't even feel it then anyway.

I reduced gravity, which probably pissed the whores off. Good, payback is a bitch, bitch. They're monsters, pains in my ass. Glad Destiny and Tammy was there, I'd probably have been dead by then, along with everybody else. They'd have killed me and then each other.

I went back to *Rawhide*. "That didn't take long," Destiny said, unharnessing. "And is gravity less?"

"Yeah."

"The droppers won't like it."

"They wouldn't much care for pirates, either," I said. "Pirates would make them slaves if they could live long enough without drops. There's pirates chasing some other poor son of a bitch who they think is me. He's hauling ass and they're hauling ass and me slowing down helps *us*. When I see a battle I'll haul ass. I masered Bill, he's behind us, hope he can get around."

And right then Bill answered. "What should we do, old buddy? I'm on batteries! The best I can do is a quarter gravity."

"Arm all your shit and dock with my boat if you're close enough so you can have a little more speed, and we'll try to sneak past when they're attacking that other company's boat."

"No, lets not dock, we won't get that much more speed and we could damage the docking rings. Those poor pirates!" he said. Bill had seen me in action and was probably grinning right then; he was too far for video, at least with our equipment.

"Fuck all them God damned pirates," I growled. God damned sons of bitches. I fucking *hate* pirates. I've lost too many friends because of the murdering bastards.

My holo showed more EMF; a battle. No time to dock the boats, anyway. "Hit it, Bill," I said. "I'll follow."

"Roger."

Destiny asked how long it would take.

175

"I don't know," I said. "You need to strap back down." I kissed her and went back to the pilot room.

I gradually increased power while Bill gave his boat all it had, which wasn't much, being on batteries and all. We were doing maybe point two gravities, if that. I followed. I saw, thankfully, that they were still battling the boat they thought was mine and I almost kind of felt sorry for the poor bastard the pirates were after because they thought he was me.

Lucky pirates. For now. I was pissed and I hate pirates anyway, like I said they've killed good friends of mine. Yeah, getting pissed is unprofessional but professionals went to college and I ain't, so fuck you, I'm retiring anyway. Now shut the fuck up before I just walk out of here, there ain't nothing you can do to me.

Yeah, asshole? Prove it.

Okay, I accept your fucking apology. Now shut the fuck up and let me finish this God damned thing so I can go buy a ring for Destiny. Where the hell was I?

Oh yeah, me and Bill was trying to sneak past the God damned pirates and get to Mars alive. Anyway, I told everybody it was safe to unstrap. It was all right for quite a few hours, but they must have finally boarded that other company's boat, and no doubt killed its captain and commandeered his ship for their own use. Poor bastard, I felt sorry for him.

It looked like me and Bill was okay, at least for now. I went back to Destiny and my movie.

Huh? Christ, guys, what does it matter? It was a show about driving cattle across the ancient American west. And God damn it, I'm hungry and I'm getting some God damned lunch. Excuse me.

What? You're all hungry, too? Well, okay, a hamburger and brogs and a glass of Shike will do for me. Yeah, with caffeine. Thanks.

I put a plug in my ear to hear the pirate traffic without bothering Destiny and still be able to hear the show myself.

Huh? Really? You never heard of it before? Jees, guys, a lot of the greats that shaped culture for well over half a century had a hand in it. The art form was in its infancy then, barely half a century old. Go watch it, there's a series of 'em, just pull the library up on your tablet, it's there. I guess Destiny's wearing off on me, she's big on movie history. Actually, she likes history, period.

Anyway, when that was over Destiny put a really silly one on, an old two dimensional movie that was hilarious. I don't think I ever laughed at puns before. I don't remember the movie's name, sorry, but there was one place where a woman wearing a dress is on a ladder with a man looking up saying "nice beaver." She says "Thanks, I just had it stuffed!" and then hands the guy a stuffed animal, a beaver a taxidermist had worked on. I laughed my ass off all the way through – at least, until the pirates realized they'd boarded the wrong boat and knew I was still alive.

Shit. I'd hoped they'd been fooled. They must not have been. I wonder how they figured it out.

They knew I was alive, wanted me dead, and had an extra ship, full of whatever cargo the boat was carrying. I hoped it wasn't weapons. I'm glad it wasn't one of ours, not just because I work for the company but because we have the best boats and especially the best weapons. Guys from the other companies are always bitching about their crappy boats and especially about their crappy weapons, but they get paid better than we do and they say the robots on their boats make okay coffee.

We were stealthy, but you can't erase everything. Ion engines leave ion trails, and they were after us. At the rate they were traveling they'd catch up to us in maybe twelve hours. We were in trouble. I was in for some serious trouble, because if I lived through this I was going to be in some deep trouble with the company because of what I had in mind.

I got back on the PA. "I'm sorry, ladies, but everyone is confined to quarters because of an emergency that's come up.

You will need to strap down again at about seven forty five tomorrow morning, I'll let you know over the PA when we need to strap down. If you get hungry, call the computer and it will send food to you. If you're not home now, you have fifteen minutes to get there."

The doorbell rang, it was Tammy. "John, I have to be able to treat the droppers," she said.

"You're not confined, that's just to help keep them under control until we can speed back up. Just pretend you sneaked out or something. Have a robot deliver drops if you can."

"What's the emergency?" she asked.

"I can't talk about it right now."

"Okay, I'll adjust the dosage so they'll sleep through most of the low gravity," she said, and left.

We watched the end of the movie but I didn't laugh much after that. It was still early but I was going to need a good night's sleep.

Chapter Thirty Nine

Interception

I had the computer wake me up at six so I'd be ready for the pirates. Of course, when the alarm went off I thought "damned whores" until I looked and was reminded that I'd set the alarm myself. I started coffee, took my shower, and ate a quick breakfast. Huh? Steak, egg, and cheese wrap. A small one.

Then I went downstairs to do a quick inspection of the engines and generator. Thankfully, nothing was broken or being worked on and everything was all right except number seventeen and the port generator. I only did a cursory check looking for red or yellow lights. I usually spend two or three hours down there checking readings, sometimes a lot longer if there's trouble, but the most time I had then was forty five minutes or so.

I went back to my quarters and checked the holo map; they'd be here in forty five minutes. That would be about quarter after eight.

Destiny was awake by then, so I had coffee with her while she ate and we watched the news. Nothing new in the news. More people dead in orbit around Venus and everyone on the station was sick. Cops had tried to arrest a nest of Pirates in San Diego, but ten cops and two pirates died and fifteen cops and five pirates were hospitalized. The rest got away, more than fifty of them.

About quarter 'til eight I went to the pilot room with a cup and a full pot of coffee, and at eight I did my normal checkouts. Good, everything was okay.

At five after eight I picked up the fone and addressed the PA system. "Strap down, ladies," I announced. "Gravity changes in two minutes and it's going to be dangerous." I masered Bill to change course and gave him coordinates to change to and had the computers lazily turn the boat around and head towards the pirates.

I lifted us to point eight nine gravity, the best I could do on one generator. Better than pirate boats can do, unless they've captured some of ours, which I didn't think was very damned likely.

They took chase when they saw me, and I turned around and headed to Mars on a different course, one that wouldn't take us anywhere near Bill's boat. The droppers were going to be happy, even though it was an hour later when I changed course again to a more direct route towards Mars and dropped it to half a gravity, a bit more than we'd been going before eight but we needed to go that fast to outrun the pirates.

I unstrapped and went back to my quarters, and alerted passenger and cargo that it was safe to unstrap.

"John, you need to talk to Tammy," Destiny said.

"Huh? Why? Talk to her about what?"

"Pirates and droppers!" she said. I didn't get it. "Look," she said, "Tammy has a last ditch weapon; you read her book and didn't get it but it's clear to me what she can do. Tell her about the pirates, I promised you I wouldn't. I know even telling me about any danger was against the book and I understand, but she might wind up saving our lives. I'd say she has an operational need to know."

Women. "You're right, I don't get it," I admitted, "and it looks like you have an idea. Talk to Tammy for me, would you? No restrictions, I trust her. But I still don't get it."

"Christ, John, you can really be dense sometimes but at least you know you can be. Why can't you understand? *These women are incredibly dangerous!* I can't believe you read that book and missed that!"

"I know they're dangerous, but they're a danger to you and me and themselves and the boat, not the pirates."

"Tammy's a psychologist and an anthropologist, dumbass. She can handle these women!"

She's right, I'm a dumbass. I don't know why she likes me so much. I still didn't get it, though, how in the hell can anybody handle a redeye monster? Christ, tasers only piss them off more and bullets only work if you hit an artery or a vital organ, and there weren't any guns inside the ship, anyway.

"Okay, okay," I said. "I told you, talk to her. I hope we don't get boarded," although I still didn't see what she had in mind.

"Boarded? You said we were safe! She might be our last chance if they actually manage to board," Destiny said. "That's what I was talking about."

"Yeah, usually we're okay but shit happens, you know? I like to be as prepared as I can. They'd need a hell of a lot more boats than are after us to do it, and they can't catch us, anyway."

She kissed me. "What you lack in education you make up for in wisdom," she said. I have no idea what she meant by it. "Look, I'm going to see Tammy, try not to get into any trouble."

I laughed. "Want to watch something when I get... SHIT!" My fone was alerting me; pirates ahead of me. How the hell did that happen?

"Destiny," I yelled, "Pirates ahead!"

She laughed. "Poor pirates!" she said. I didn't get it.

I went to the pilot room, calling Bill over the maser with my fone. "Bill, we got pirates, see 'em?" I didn't know how far away he was, and hoped he was too far away to hear me or to get picked up on the pirate's radar; our boats are stealthy but can be seen if you're close enough. "Go to zero gravity if you can hear me and they haven't spotted you so you won't leave an ion trail, I'm gonna nuke the sons of bitches."

I switched to the PA system. "Strap down, ladies, weird gravity almost immediately. We don't need nobody getting hurt today."

Rather than changing my heading away from them, I kept on course to intercept. Yeah, I learned that word in boat training. And yeah, this was strictly against company regulations, but fuck regulations. I was in way too much danger from my cargo to have to worry about a bunch of God damned pirates, too.

Ten or fifteen seconds later I got a "roger" from Bill, he must have been pretty damned close. He should have been way away by now, did that damned fool follow me or was it orbital mechanics? Orbital mechanics is way over my head.

Ten minutes later the pirates were coming towards me. I grinned. Poor bastards... die, you motherfuckers! I dropped my atomic right when it would be in the middle of them, and made the boat's portholes, which were all in the bow on the ceiling, turn black. Not sure how this shit works but it works. I plan on going to college.

Gravity got a little weird, of course, but not near as much as I thought I'd have to make it.

That bunch was easy, the blast from that one atomic got all of them... but there would be more, I was sure of it. There were half a dozen pirate gangs and they all hated each other, but they hated us so much more that sometimes they would band together. This was probably one of them times.

Chapter Forty

Boarded!

Me and Bill hauled ass out of there towards Mars as fast as his crippled boat would take him. I did another inspection because first, I hadn't done a full inspection yet that day, second because I'd pushed her pretty hard, and third because I sure didn't need any new surprises. We were at a third gravity because of Bill, and he was having a hard time keeping up. A third gravity? On batteries? I need to have him teach me some of that nerd shit. I'd given up on docking; if we did run across pirates I'd need to fight, and you can't do much maneuvering when you're docked.

The whores wouldn't like the low gravity a bit, so I tried to stay away from them.

I trudged down all those damned steps to my "dungeon" to inspect the engines and generators. Engine seventeen and the port generator were still not working, of course, but everything else was shipshape. Amazing since I'd been pushing them pretty hard.

On the way back to our quarters there were fifty whores in the commons all arguing. Damn it, Tammy! But we *were* at Mars gravity, maybe a little less. As I was cursing Tammy in my head she came towards me. "Damn it, Tammy!" I said. "The whores sound like they ain't got no drops. I don't need this, not now. There's pirates."

"They're going to get the minimum. The low gravity is helping, too. You'll thank me."

"I'll thank you? For a boat full of pissed off droppers?"

"Yeah," she said. "For a boatload of pissed off droppers.

I've learned an awful lot about them on this trip, much more than we can learn on Earth. Now if you'll excuse me I have to go play dope dealer. Just hope my calculations are accurate." She walked towards the commons.

I didn't get it. What kind of calculations? Well, screw it. I went back to our quarters.

"Took you long enough," Destiny said. "Are the pirates gone?"

"Yeah," I answered, "I had to inspect the engines. The pirates are gone for now, I killed 'em. Loosed an atomic on 'em. I'm sorry you're on this boat, Destiny, 'cause I'm scared. They surely hate me so much now they'll be willing to give up my ship and cargo to kill me."

"They don't know what your cargo is. John, if they don't blow us up..."

"I don't think they can," I said. "In fact, I'm pretty sure they can't. An atomic can't even damage us unless it goes off less than two hundred meters away. But with enough vessels they could board us. If they do that we're all dead. I'm more scared for you than I am for me."

"John," she said, "don't worry about them boarding us, if they try we'll be fine. Jesus but you're dense sometimes. Didn't you read Tammy's book?"

"Yeah, but it didn't say anything about pirates."

"Shut up and start the movie, dumbass, you'll see. Jesus, John. These girls are dangerous when they don't have drops!"

"Yeah, and it makes it worse for me."

"God damn it, John..." she said before the alarm rang and interrupted her.

"God damn whores," I said. Destiny followed me out.

There was a melee in the commons. Shit, I thought Tammy was going to give them whores drops.

When I got there, Tammy was on a medic with blood trickling from the side of her mouth. Those things are fast! It already had a blood pressure cuff around her arm and something on her head, I'm not sure what, I ain't no doctor.

And the whores were fighting over the drops Tammy had brought; I didn't know it then, but it was because she didn't want them horny and sleepy, she wanted them mean. I still couldn't understand why.

I can really be a dumbass sometimes.

The medic took her to the sick bay with Destiny following Tammy and the robot, and I pulled out my fone and locked the door to the commons. Shit. "Computer," I said to the fone, "flood the commons with, uh..." damn, what was the name of that stuff again? "Computer, what gas will, uh, cause the people in the commons to, uh... lose consciousness?"

"An inert gas will..."

"Computer, list inert gasses."

"Nitrogen, Helium..."

"Flood the commons with nitrogen and open the door when the people are all, uh, unconscious. And have a robot bring plastic handcuffs, about a hundred."

"Acknowledged."

A few minutes later the door opened, and I went in and put plastic handcuffs on them, wrists and ankles. Damn, hundreds of years after they were invented and there's nothing cheaper or works better.

Then I went to talk to Tammy. I hoped she wasn't hurt too bad.

The readout on the medic said she had a slight concussion, but not too serious. She was still unconscious. I said to Destiny "Do me a favor, hon. Please. Go make sure the whores I roped stay alive."

"What? John, what did you do?"

"There were fifty or more of them fighting over not enough drops for everybody. I don't have a clue what Tammy was thinking but they knocked her cold and fought over the drops. I knocked them out and tied them with plastic cuffs."

"How can I keep them alive?"

"Find some drops," I said. And Tammy had woke up, it looked like.

185

"No!" she exclaimed. "Half a dose each. We need 'em mean!"

"Got it," Destiny said. I still didn't get it. Tammy gave her a dropper from her pocket and said "Here's a weak dose. One drop in one eye only!"

Destiny said "got it" again and hurried off.

"I don't get it," I said. "Can you explain..." and the damned alarm interrupted me again. More fucking pirates. Lots of 'em.

Shit. "Take care of the whores as soon as the medic lets you," I said, and ran to the pilot room.

This was a bitch. The medic would keep Tammy from getting thrown around, but any sudden maneuvering would throw Destiny and the tied up whores all over the place; you need to be strapped in for that kind of shit. So I gave it all my lone generator had, and prayed. And I'm not even religious, I was just scared shitless. I called Destiny. "Hon, you have to strap down. Now. Forget the whores."

"No!" she said. "Only three more!"

"God damn it, Destiny, we have less than five minutes, we're surrounded by them. They're coming from all directions. It's like a swarm of bees."

"That's all I need," she said. "Tell the women to strap down!"

I did. And launched a dozen EMPs and an atomic, all the while spewing deadly radiation from the still-working generator. Then I did a lazy turn and did it again. Must have disabled dozens of ships, maybe hundreds, but these damned things were swarming. Destiny called. "Everyone's secured."

Good. Now I could maneuver, and maneuver I did. I'm sure maids were busy cleaning up puke and piss afterwards because gravity was *really* weird for quite a while. I made my boat into an outer space roller coaster.

But God damn it, there were too many of them. One ship latched on to the port airlock. Fuck, I was a dead man. I ran to the port side docking bay, above the crippled generator and one room over from machine storage, leaping down the stairs at almost full gravity.

I couldn't maneuver with that mass on my side anyway. At least I could slow down a boarding party. But I was going to be dead anyway, and so was everybody else. But I had an idea... I could at least kill these assholes and they wouldn't be able to use this docking ring, at least if I was lucky.

I was in the storage area before they could get through the airlock. Thank God for small miracles, I guess. God, get me through this and I'll go to church every damned Sunday for a whole year! I swear! My heart was pounding, from running and from being scared, and sweat was pouring off of me; we were still close to a full gravity.

I moved a huge battery from storage to the docking bay next to the airlock and worked on it as they tried to get through the airlock. Damn but I was scared, of the pirates and of what I was doing. I was actually more scared of what I was doing than I was of the pirates.

What I was doing was making a really big battery into a really big bomb. Bill showed me how to do that years ago, I told you he was kind of a nerd. It really wasn't all that hard, since training was about how to *not* turn batteries into explosives. Those things hold a hell of a lot of energy.

I wired it into the light panel. Turn on the light from the storage room and BOOM! Dead pirates.

I barely got out and locked the next bulkhead that separated the docking room from storage before they got through the lock, and I flipped the switch after they were all inside.

They all died. Good. It blew their ship away from mine. Bad. That meant the next wave would have an easy entrance, since there wasn't any thing blocking the door and no way to lock it; they had ruined the airlock's security lock. So much for praying. I was hoping their boat docked to mine would... oh, hell. I ran up the flight of stairs as fast as I could run. I had to get to the pilot room and steer this tub.

When I left the storage area and went into the hallway my worst nightmare was waiting for me. Two hundred dropheads, pissed off dropheads without any drops and with those scary bloodshot eyes, although they weren't as red as that one woman's had been, all with big knives.

I was a dead man. I was sure of it.

"You stole our drops!" and similar stuff, they yelled and screamed, coming at me with those damned knives. I stood there like a stone, petrified.

And they all stormed past me, like they didn't even see me! What the hell?

Tammy and Destiny were drinking coffee in the commons, seeming to be completely not worried at all about pirates. Jesus but educated people can be stupid. I went to the pilot room, but it was too late – another pirate boat had docked. Damn it!

And then... nothing happened. No pirates. What the fuck? It fell off the ship and another one docked... and another, and another. Five hundred times! Holy crap! What the hell, they had to be running out of bad guys by now, five hundred pirate ships all full of pirates. Christ!

This had been going on for days. I was too damned busy trying to dodge pirates and shoot at them to try and figure it out. I have a lot of guns to shoot, fifty lasers and eight rail guns, and I spent days marking targets for the computer to destroy. But I couldn't dodge them because cargo wasn't strapped in so I couldn't do anything fancy and they didn't take over the boat and I couldn't figure out why not. I didn't get any sleep at all, except two or three times when I passed out in the pilot seat despite all the coffee I was drinking. If I ate I don't remember what. I'm not sure I did eat.

The fleet finally showed up. By then most of the rail gun projectiles and all my atomics were exhausted, and so was I. There were hundreds of abandoned and disabled pirate ships scattered across the solar system, or at least part of the way from Earth to Mars, and the few hundred pirate ships that hadn't tried to board hauled ass out of there, with half of the company's destructor fleet on their asses. How about that, they had one, after all. So why are there still pirates?

I still didn't know why the pirates hadn't overrun the boat. Destiny and Tammy were still drinking coffee in the commons, with about a dozen stoned, naked whores laying around the big room. I hadn't slept on purpose for days and was living on coffee. I wondered if they were, too.

I sat down and poured another cup of coffee. I was so full of coffee my hands were shaking so hard it wasn't easy to hold the cup still enough to drink. "I need a bath and a nap," I said. "What the hell just happened?"

"Jesus but you're a dumbass," Tammy said. "You read my book and you still didn't get it. John, get it through your head – these women are damned dangerous. I told them the pirates stole my drops before they hit me."

I finally got it. "Have to hand it to you," I said. "I guess they were one hell of a weapon!"

"You guess?" Destiny said. "John!"

I blushed. "No, they were one hell of a weapon. And you controlled it well, Tammy."

"Hey, asshole, me too," Destiny said, grinning.

"Yeah, you too. I'm stupid. Why do you like me so much?"

"Because you know what a dumbass you are," she said, grinning even wider. I was crestfallen.

"Oh, come on, you big baby, we're still getting married, aren't we?"

"Well yeah," I said, "If you still want to marry a dumbass."

"Excuse us," Destiny said to Tammy, and took my hand and started to lead me back to our cabin. I almost threw the nearly full coffee cup in the trash. I was really tired and wasn't thinking straight, completely forgetting that I had to inspect downstairs again; it hadn't been inspected in two days and I'd really been pushing it.

I also forgot about the monsters.

Chapter Forty One

Monsters

"Hold on, Destiny," Tammy said, "we're still in trouble."

I got it. Finally, even being so tired that my brain wasn't working right. God, what a dumbass I was! I really needed some sleep, but I wasn't going to get any for a while.

"Computer, lock all doors," I said. "She's right, Destiny, We're in trouble. I finally get it. She left them short of drops and told them the pirates stole them. They're not even human any more, you should have seen them. They scared the hell out of me with those crazy red eyes and all those knives and their eyes weren't even very red yet. Jesus, my boat is full of inhuman monsters!"

"John!" Destiny said. "How can you talk like that? They're *people!*"

"John's right," Tammy said. "they aren't. Only Lek and the ones in here that had squirreled enough away that they wouldn't go through withdrawal are human, and these girls are only barely human. John, you might not be very educated but you're not stupid. Destiny, he's right, they're not human. They don't even know about drops right now. We need to find a way to get this drug into their systems and..."

"What if we can't?" Destiny asked.

"Then everybody's dead. We have to find a way. A spray bottle of drops won't help anything against all of them. John, is there any way to send vapors of it into the atmosphere?"

I shook my head. "If there is I don't know how."

Destiny said "If we can't get the drugs in them, we can use John's houseboat to escape at least, since the droppers will kill everyone and die anyway. We can ride back on one of the fleet's boats."

Tammy said "Just getting to the houseboat would be incredibly dangerous, but I don't really see any other way, either."

"I'm afraid they'll find a way in here anyway," I said. "They shouldn't have been able to get through the stairwell doors but they did, even starting to go through withdrawal."

"I did that," Destiny said. "I told the computer to unlock the door."

"You can do that?" I asked, perplexed.

"John, my dad started this company, and I hold more stock than anybody but him or Charles. There isn't a company door anywhere I can't open with a word. How did you think I got outside the ship? But we have to get to that pilot room!"

"Hold on," I said. "No, it's way too dangerous and we won't have to. I have an idea the computer gave me earlier when Angel thought she lost her drops down the drain." I pulled out my fone, forgetting I'd already ordered the computer to lock all the doors. I *really* needed some sleep! "Computer, lock and seal all doors, especially the door to the commons and my quarters and Doctor Winter's cabin and the pilot room."

The computer replied "All doors have been locked for the last five minutes. Sealing doorways." I was *really* sleepy... and scared.

"What good will that do, dumbass?" Tammy asked. "You might as well lock the doors against a herd of elephants that are holding sharks with friggin' lasers!"

"Huh?" I said.

Destiny laughed. "We haven't watched that one yet, Tammy. What are you thinking, John?"

I said "I'm thinking Tammy knows drug addicted whores but I know my boat and its computers. Now shush, both of you. I know what I'm doing.

"Computer!" I said into my fone, "replace all air in

every room except the commons with nitrogen. And have robots bring three small oxygen bottles and masks to the commons."

"John," Tammy said, "you're not a dumbass, that was a stroke of genius! That's how you controlled Angel and the ones that attacked me. I wondered how you did that. Are you sure you haven't gone to college?"

"I don't get it," Destiny said.

"You didn't take many biology courses, did you?"

"Not after undergrad, and not much then even. Why?"

Tammy laughed. "Of course not. What does an astrophysicist have to know about biology?"

I said "I thought you said you were an astronomer?"

"I hold degrees in both. There's really been no difference in the last hundred years, anyway, John. Astronomers have to know an awful lot of physics and chemistry. But Tammy's right, no biology. So what's going on and why am I scared to death and you guys seem to be fine?"

Tammy said "John's smarter than I thought he was. I knew he was no dummy, even though he isn't educated. But that was really a stroke of genius, and I'm embarrassed I didn't think of it."

"Think of what?"

"Nitrogen is an inert gas," Tammy explained.

"Yeah, I knew that," Destiny said. "Undergrad shit. Basic chemistry. So what?"

"It isn't poisonous, like carbon dioxide. They won't even know there's no oxygen, they'll just get light headed or high or something like that, and go to sleep. Then we put on the oxygen masks John told the robots to fetch, put a couple drops in their eyes, and make the atmosphere normal before they get brain damage from lack of oxygen."

"What?" Destiny said. "There are two hundred of them!"

"Relax," I said. "Once they pass out we'll add oxygen to the nitrogen so there won't be brain damage. Once we get drops in all their eyes we'll set the atmosphere to normal and they'll all wake up happy. Will they remember any of it, Tammy?" I asked, curious.

"Not much," she replied. "Certainly nothing after they stopped being human."

"What do you mean, 'stopped being human'?" Destiny asked. "You guys keep saying that!"

"God, Destiny," Tammy said, "when you're out of your field you're even dumber than John!"

I didn't know whether to feel insulted or complimented.

She continued. "A wolf with rabies is more sentient than an angel tear addict going through withdrawal. You know those old gray movies we used to watch about vampires and werewolves?"

"Huh?" I said. "You guys have known each other for a long time?"

"We went to college together. Now, shut up, John," Destiny said. "Go on, Tammy."

"Is a werewolf human? A vampire?" she asked.

"Of course not."

"So where does a vampire come from?"

"Come on, Tammy. A vampire bites a human and he turns into a vampire himself."

"Is he human?"

"No, he's a vampire."

"But was he human?"

"Yeah."

"So were the droppers. But not now. Like a vampire, or a werewolf. Only this isn't some sort of supernatural hocus-pocus stupid movie voodoo, it's chemistry. This is real. These women are worse than vampires or werewolves. They look human, except for those eyes, but they're not. I thought you'd read the literature?"

Destiny blushed. "I did. I guess I just didn't get it."

Tammy grinned. "John got it. You two dumbasses are perfect for each other."

Destiny said "Shouldn't we start now?"

"Too dangerous," Tammy said. "Wait until they've passed out. How long, John?"

I laughed. "You're the scientist, all I know about knocking droppers out with nitrogen is what the computer told me." My brain was actually working despite the lack of sleep. Wow. Adrenaline, I guess. "Computer," I said into my fone, "how long until all cargo are unconscious?"

"All cargo will not become unconscious under present conditions for foreseeable time frame" the stupid, stubborn piece of junk computer said.

"Computer, explain!" God damned computer.

"One specimen is in a protected area," the computer said.

Stupid damned computers. Why in the hell do they act like that? I sighed. "Okay, dumbass computer, excepting the single specimen how long?"

"One minute," it said. What? Damned computer, would it take one minute or did it mean it had to compute something? God damned computers.

"Computer, inform me when all but the 'specimen' in the commons are aslee... I mean, unconscious." It replied with the expected "Affirmative." And then another damned alarm went off as gravity seemed to get lighter.

God damn it, there isn't enough damned money on the solar system to pay me for this shit. I'm retiring, I've had it.

If I live, anyway, I thought. I have two hundred vampires and werewolves on board. Drugula, I guess.

Shit. The other damned generator went out. And I couldn't do another inspection until we got drops in the werewolves' eyes and made the atmosphere normal.

And I *really* needed some sleep really bad.

Chapter Forty Two

Nitrous

I pulled out my fone and called the fleet commander, who I was amazingly boss of, and told him about our little power problem, then asked the computer what the robots were doing about repairs. Or tried to, anyway.

"Computer, what is the, uh... status of..." and the God damned machine interrupted me, of course. Who programs this junk anyway?

"All cargo unconscious except specimen in commons area. Danger to cargo."

"Computer," I told the piece of shit, "God damn it, how much oxygen will keep them alive and asl... uh, unconscious without damaging them?"

"The percentage is..."

"Add it, you piece of shit!" Yeah, getting pissed at a machine is really smart, ain't it? But I really needed sleep. "Computer. Where are them fucking robots?"

The stupid thing replied "Robots have no sex and do not engage in..."

Jesus. "Computer, where are the..."

A robot carrying oxygen bottles and masks came in, the door opening quickly, it entering quickly, and the doors closing really damned fast. I thought nitrogen was harmless? It turned out that the nitrogen wouldn't hurt us but monsters would; they were all outside the commons trying to get in to kill us and eat us. We would have been dead if we'd tried to get to the houseboat.

We got to work making the vampires and werewolves

and frankensteins and whatever the hell kind of other monsters these damned dropheads were back into humans, or something not really all that different from humans, again. Some had some pretty bad cuts, we gave them their drops first and then medics took them to sick bay to treat them. I ordered the computer to put normal air in sick bay.

Poor broads. I really feel sorry for them. I hope Destiny's charity can help them, it sure looked like Tammy was getting results from Lek. Lek was wearing clothes and acting like a respectable lady, although her eyes were usually a little bloodshot and she wasn't smiling much, especially for someone who came from the Land of Smiles.

That God damned stupid fucking computer must suck at arithmetic, because I barely got the last drop in the last monster's eye when she started waking up. Scared the shit out of me, how would you feel if you were putting eye drops in Dracula's eye and he started to wake up? Especially if he had scary red eyes like a mad dropper? Christ, I almost had a coronary!

Now I had to see what the hell was wrong with that damned generator and do a full inspection of the engines. Shit. Well, it wasn't as bad as that Saturn run when all the engines blew out, at least I had plenty of full batteries and all but one engine was working.

You guys know, of course, that you can only run fifty eight engines on batteries. That's only point twenty five gravities and usually not even that much, I don't know how Bill managed more but he's a nerd that reads a lot of technical manuals. The whores ain't gonna like it one little bit. And if more pirates come... I mean, we ain't that near to Mars yet, we have a while. I'm just glad I have that fleet. And its commander said I was in charge! Wow, I ain't never been in charge of nothing but machinery before.

Tammy called. "John, we need nitrous oxide, a precise amount, in the atmosphere. The computer said I don't have the clearance to accomplish it."

"Give me a minute," I said, and hung up. Hung? Up?

"Computer," I ordered the fone, "add whatever Doctor Winters asks for to the atmosphere." What the hell is nitrous oxide and why did Tammy want it? I called her back. "You're getting your nitr, uh... whatever. What the hell is it and why does it need to be in the atmosphere?"

"Nitrous oxide. Laughing gas. It will calm the droppers down and they won't mind the low gravity much at all."

"Will it affect us?" I asked.

"Of course it will," she answered. "What, you think it's something that only affects droppers?"

"Well, I'd hoped so. What will it do? Look, Tammy, if I can't think straight we might die. It's bad enough with me being so damned tired and sleepy, I already can't think very straight."

"I've seen you drunk on wine!" she said.

"Not when there were pirates after us and running on batteries and with another hailstorm coming that we'd been past if our only working generator hadn't broke and when I'm in charge of a God damned fleet and I ain't never been in charge of nothing before. Captains may not have to know as much as they did when they had to go to college, but we got to know when it's okay to drink and when beer will kill you. And this is one of those times. *I can't get intoxicated!*"

Intoxicated. Them two is rubbing off on me. "I can't be breathing laughing gas. It could kill us all. Because right now I need what little brain I have left."

The computer interrupted with an alarm. "Meteor shower ahead".

She thought a second... maybe not even that long. "Get an oxygen generation belt from sick bay and breathe from that. Your thought processes may even be clearer depending on how much nitrous you ingest."

"I what? 'In jest'? What's funny got to do with it?"

"Breathe. Drink. Eat. With this it's just breathe. Keep the oxygen mask on and you should be okay."

"Okay," I said, and told the computer to flood the pilot room and my quarters and Tammy's quarters and engines and generators with normal air, with Tammy's laughing gas mixture in the rest of the boat, and then I went to the pilot room to steer around the space rain, holding my breath.

After driving for fifteen or twenty minutes, by hand, no less, and I almost never do that even though I did fighting all those God damned pirates, but I had to because I was on batteries, I was around the rocks. I clipped the bottle of oxygen that a robot had brought to my belt and put on the mask. I had to see if the robots were having any luck with the generator, and I still had a hell of a lot of engines to inspect down there.

There were a hundred giggling, naked women in the commons. I guessed Tammy and Destiny were in my cabin where air was normal and they wouldn't get stoned, and that Tammy had been generous with drops. She sure knew what she was doing.

I went back down the five damned flights of stairs to the starboard generator. God, but it was a nasty, stinking, bloody mess down there, so many body parts piled in the hallway I wasn't going to be able to inspect half the engines or the other generator. Apparently the bodies and body parts had been thrown, pushed, or chased over the storage railing into the hallway with the high ceiling.

Where were the damned robots? I pulled out my fone. "Computer," I said, "why aren't there any robots working on the generator?"

It replied "Repair machinery is removing parts from the port generator that were not damaged when the generator incinerated to install in the starboard generator." I wondered how the hell they got there past the stinking mess.

"Can they fix it?"

"Negative."

"Why not?"

"We are lacking a replacement pressure regulator. Port generator pressure regulator was incinerated."

Damn. "Okay, computer, How long is it going to take to replace everything except the regulator?"

"Between one and three hours."

It sounded like time for a movie, I thought, so tired that I forgot how badly I needed to sleep. I inspected the engines and was amazed that there wasn't anything wrong with any of them after what I'd put them through. At least, the ones I could get to, bodies and parts of bodies were piled three or four meters high. I started back to my quarters, but stopped when I had an idea. I called my "second in command"; heh, how about that? Anyway, I asked Ramos "Does anybody in this fleet have a spare pressure regulator that will work on my generator?"

The answer was a "yes"; one of the boats could shut down a generator and remove the regulator, whatever the hell a "pressure regulator" is, dock, and my robots would install it. Of course I had to get paper from the company, but we had three hours. I called Ramos again and told him to to dock and supply when the paperwork came in

I left my bloody boots on the landing and walked in my stocking feet to the pilot room to send paper to the company, then went home.

We didn't even bother with dinner, we just took a shower together and then sat on the couch cuddling to Clapton. This had been one hell of a long, trying day. In fact, today had been several days long. At least tomorrow we would have normal air and better gravity.

We both fell asleep on the couch, cuddled up together.

Chapter Forty Three

Injury

We both woke up around seven, still cuddled up on the couch. We'd been asleep for fifteen hours on that thing! We cuddled a little while more, then Destiny started coffee while I took care of the ship's air and corrected the course, since I was sleeping when the generator came back online.

We took another shower together after drinking a little coffee and she told the cook to make pancakes and sausage, and we watched the news while breakfast was cooking. That robot makes pretty good pancakes. The sausage is pretty good, too, but my mom could do better.

There was nothing new on the news except Venus and pirates, and pirates sure weren't new to me. More people on the Venus station were dead and the rest weren't expected to live. That must be one nasty disease!

There was some sort of scandal where some politician was caught having financial connections to the pirates, was impeached, charged with violation of banking laws and bribery, fined, and put on probation.

I'd have shot the God damned son of a bitch, or at least put him in prison. Fucking bastard was a God damned traitor. The pirates they'd caught on Earth earlier had all been sentenced to prison, which is what led up to the politician's arrest; his pirate friends had ratted him out in hope of lighter sentences.

At eight I checked the readings, and they all checked out fine because I'd just been in there an hour earlier. Then I did inspections. I had to check the engines and generators but could only check half the engines and only the starboard generator because the hallway halfway from port to starboard was completely clogged with body parts; I couldn't check the port side engines or the busted generator. I couldn't get in port storage upstairs from the generator at all even.

It would take the maids weeks to clean up all the blood. They'd still be working on it when we got to Mars. God, but it was a nasty mess down there, and it was starting to stink *really* bad. You couldn't smell it upstairs, thank God, but going downstairs made me want to throw up. And it looked as disgusting as it smelled.

I took off my bloody boots at the top of the stairs and put on the shoes I'd worn there. I was going to need another shower.

There was a commotion in the commons on the way back to our quarters; Sparkle was in there and obviously low on drops. Dangerously low. Tammy came walking quickly up.

"So you're going to visit Sparkle?" I asked her.

"Are you fucking crazy, John? Of course I am! I must not have been clear in my book. If one of these women runs completely out of drops, we're all dead. Really. Trust me on this, this is my main field of study."

"They knocked you on your ass and stole your drops the last time."

"It was... well, a gamble. It paid off, I got knocked out but how many pirates died?"

My fone rang; it was Sandy, a chubby red haired girl, wanting to know why the maid didn't show up. Of course, they were all in the engine and generator rooms, cleaning up blood and guts and the nasty stuff that's inside guts. It really stunk bad, worse than when Billie blew herself up. Most sickening mess I've ever seen, or smelled.

I told her they were only coming half as often because of the sickening mess downstairs, and hung it up... where did that phrase "hang up" come from? And answered Tammy.

"From what I can tell, thousands."

"Where are all the bodies?"

"The robots jettisoned them. Lots of them, anyway, there are an awful lot still downstairs. Now they're all little bitty comets, except the ones that haven't been cleaned up yet. But there's still one hell of a mess down there in the engine and generator rooms and it isn't even all the way cleaned up upstairs in the port storage bay."

My fone rang again; a heavy German accent asking about the maids.

I hung up the fone after telling her and wondered again why we said "hung up", and why the damned thing was called a fone. But then, why is an apple called an apple? Why are robots called robots? I'm called John because that's the name my parents gave me. I should go to college. Maybe I should read, like Wild Bill and Destiny does.

I got on the PA and informed them that maids would only be there every other day for the duration of the trip because they would all be busy in the engine and generator rooms. I went the rest of the way back home and took another shower.

While a pizza was cooking we watched another *Star Wars* movie because the first one was so funny, but we only got to see twenty minutes or so before an alarm went off: Injury to passenger.

"Pause it and come on," I said, hurrying to the door. "Tammy's hurt." I talked to the fone. "Where is Tamatha Winters?"

It said "Cargo eighty seven."

"Is she alone?"

"Affirmative." Damned computers.

"Is a medic on the way?"

"Medic en route." Why did this thing type "en route"? Why not "in route"? I ain't French.

"Where's Sparkle?"

"Unable to process order or question, please rephrase." God damned piece of shit computer! Who programs these damned things, anyway?

"Where, is, Sparkle?" I repeated.

"The term 'sparkle' does not exist in the database except as a dictionary entry."

Shit. "Destiny, what's Sparkle's real name?"

"I don't know."

Shit. "What are you going to do?" she asked.

"I don't know," I said. I could find Sparkle's picture in the computer but it would take too long to go through two hundred pictures.

"Is doctor Winters in sick bay?"

"Affirmative."

Damned computers. "Condition?" I asked.

"Critical," it said, and Destiny got pale. I probably got pale, too. There was no way Destiny and me could handle those dropheads without Tammy.

I had an idea; I'd done this before but decided to look for Sparkle before knocking all of the droppers out; I don't want to damage cargo, let alone hurt people.

"We need to find Sparkle," I said. She went looking down one hallway and I looked down another. "Computer," I said, "when I say so I want you to replace all air except here and the sick bay with nitrogen and inform me when everyone in, uh," damned computers, "the affected areas are asl... uh, unconscious."

"Affirmative," it said. Stupid computer.

It only took a few minutes to find her; she was in the commons noisily attacking the two Thai girls who had the same names. I thought it looked like she wanted to eat them, as in take them apart and swallow their flesh like a cannibal or a lion or a wolf or something, and her eyes weren't even all the way red yet. Her eyes were still really bloodshot and scary, though. The gruesome picture of the generators and all along the halls by the engines haunted me; it looked like some of the remaining flesh had been partially eaten. There were even bones with teeth marks on them. Nasty. But the two Thai girls were holding their own; I didn't know it but both were professional martial arts instructors. Lek told me later they practiced Thai kickboxing. I have no idea how they got hooked on drops. They were easy to tell apart, now that one of them had started wearing clothes.

I had the computer shut the door and flood it with nitrogen and hoped Sparkle passed out before the Thai girls did. When they did I had two medics bring the Thai girls out and I cuffed Sparkle, wrists and ankles. Then I went to Tammy's quarters in search of drops; angel tears were all that was going to save all of our lives now.

I looked everywhere. She'd hid them real good, because I couldn't find them after looking for an hour and a half, so I called Destiny. She didn't know where she kept them, either.

Shit. We were all dead.

Maybe not. I'd had Lek, the Thai girl who talked kind of all right and knocked me out (I think, I'm not sure) but was acting human these days who I'd had took to sick bay. The other Thai girl hadn't been injured but the one that talks good was still unconscious and sporting a black eye.

If Sparkle didn't get her drug she was going to die horribly and if she wasn't chained down we were all going to die horribly, and maybe even if she was chained down we'd still all die horribly.

I went to the sick bay to see Tammy and Lek, hoping Tammy was going to live. Her medic said she was stable, but she still wasn't awake. I guess stable is better than critical, which is what she was before, but I ain't no doctor. The whole side of her face was purple.

Destiny was there. "John," she said, "Shit, what are we going to do?"

"I don't know," I said. "If Lek wakes up maybe we can save Sparkle and if Tammy wakes up maybe we can save everybody, but without those drops we're all dead."

Lek stirred a little. "Give her time," Destiny said. "Let her wake up."

But she was already sitting up on the medic, ripping off the oxygen mask. "Sparkle need drops! She be animal! She no have drops she die! We all die!"

"I know," I said. "But we don't have any. Do you have some?"

"I no want be animal and dealer hurt real bad," she said, glancing at Tammy. "All I got is all I got!"

"You're lucid," Destiny said. What the hell does lucid mean? "If Tammy dies we're all dead, you can see that. Now we're trying to save Sparkle. We don't want anyone going through withdrawal. How much would it take to save Sparkle and how much do you have?"

"I no have enough," she said. "I be animal before I get to Mars."

I got mean; this was one of those God damned times I really hate, when I had to be an asshole just to keep people from dying.

"Lek, what you got is what you got unless you're willing to share. And you know what you got won't get you all the way to Mars, we'll all be dead first. I'll tie you up and let you die from withdrawal if you won't help Sparkle."

"You would not do that!"

"Watch me, bitch. My job is getting all of us to Mars alive, or at least as many of us as possible. Now where are your God damned drops and how much does Sparkle need?"

She pulled out a bottle, one of the kinds with a dropper for a cap. "She only need one drop now, only in one eye, give rest back, okay? I no want be animal."

"Thank you," I said, "I'll give you your bottle back. I know that's why you want to go to Mars. You don't want to be a dropper."

"I want be human again," she said. "I not dropper, I drophead. I no want be animal. I hope Tammy wake up or we all dead."

Yeah, me too.

We would be okay if Tammy woke up in time, but she

was still in a coma when it was time for bed. At least the medic's readout had said her "condition was upgraded to fair".

Chapter Forty Four

Awake

I woke up about quarter after seven, and Destiny was already up and had coffee started. "Hungry?" She asked.

"Yeah, I am. Did we even eat dinner last night? Did you tell the robots to start breakfast?"

"No, I wanted to try something new for breakfast and wanted to see what you wanted to eat first. You know I'm a history buff, well, I found a really old recipe in the computer called a 'breakfast horse shoe'. They used to have them in the twentieth and twenty first centuries in a city in the American midwest."

"A horse shoe? That doesn't sound too appetizing, What's in it?" I asked.

"Well, the recipe I found calls for ham or pork sausage, but turkey or beef or chicken or almost any kind of meat will do. It's a piece of toast covered with cheese, with meat on the cheese, more cheese on the meat, scrambled eggs on the cheesy meat, cheese on that, hash browns on that and more cheese on top of the hash browns.

"They had dinner horse shoes as well. Those didn't have eggs, and had french fries instead of hash browns."

"Sounds cheesy," I said. "Sure, I'll try one."

She took a shower while the robots made horse shoes. No shower for me yet today, I was going to need one when I was done with inspecting that nasty mess downstairs anyway.

I only had enough time to finish half of my horse shoe, but I had to go to work.

That horse shoe was pretty good. The recipe was so old I

was surprised it was in the database, but Destiny probably brought her own history database along. She really likes history, and she's getting me interested in it, too.

All of the readouts were okay in the pilot room, except for that I probably wouldn't be able to inspect those hundred and twenty two engines that I still hadn't been able to get to because of all the nastiness blocking the halls.

Number seventeen was of course still not working, and it was one of the ones I couldn't get to. That didn't really matter, though, because I'd be damned if I was going to light it again, even if the robots could fix it without melting.

Maybe the maids had paths cleared out by now so I could inspect the rest, they'd made lots of progress when I was down there yesterday.

No way was I going to inspect cargo today no matter what that damned book says, that would have been crazy fucking stupid dangerous. Some of the dropheads might be low on drops and there's no way I'm inspecting a monster's pen. Fuck that God damned book, I wasn't going to do it.

I went to inspect the sick bay first. Tammy was still in a coma, and I was worried. What were the droppers going to do when they woke up?

The maids had indeed jettisoned a lot more of the gross, nasty mess and I was able to get through the halls and inspect almost all the engines this morning, although there was still a hell of a lot of stinking gore and I still couldn't get to the generator or ten engines.

There was a different robot working on seventeen, with a smashed up robot next to it, probably damaged in the excitement. Damn it, I wanted that damned engine left alone, we didn't need any more melted robots. I unplugged it, took a lead off of the battery that powered the robot and plugged it back in, hoping another damned robot wouldn't reconnect the battery. Anyway, I trudged back up those damned stairs. As I was climbing stairs I foned the computer and told it to "alert me when Doctor Winters regains consciousness." The stupid computers, they only understand military nerd talk. I took my filthy boots off at the landing at the top of the stairs, it was still really gross down there. I took my shower when I got home.

Destiny and me had roast beef sandwiches and fried potatoes and salad for lunch. I was starved, I'd only had time for half my breakfast and that was probably my first full real meal since yesterday morning. I don't think we ate that pizza we ordered for lunch the day before.

While we were eating, the alarm went off; Tammy was awake. Thank God! Both of us took off at a run toward the sick bay. I told the robots not to clear the table, if I didn't the stupid things would throw the rest of my lunch away.

She was sitting up on the medic with the oxygen mask still on her face and the needle still in her arm. She was taking the mask off, looking a little groggy. "The droppers!" she said, her speech a little slurred.

"I know," Destiny said. "Tell me where the drops are and lay back down, you had a serious concussion. You've been out for two days and we're worried about the droppers."

"You two can't handle them," she said.

"We have to," I replied. "you can't."

"You could overdose them!"

"Better than underdosing," I said.

"Not much. Look, John, there is a trunk in my quarters with a false bottom, the drops are in there. They're in small bottles and there are plenty. Just put one bottle in each addict's quarters when you do inspection and I'll adjust dosage later when the gurney lets me go."

"Okay," I said. "What do I do if one is starting to go through withdrawal?"

"Drop the bottle and run like hell!"

That seemed logical to me. Hell, opening the door and just tossing a bottle in seemed even more logical, these girls were freaky scary without drops. Scarier than Destiny's old gray horror movies, even.

"We'll be back when we're done," Destiny said.

There was a melee in the commons. I locked the door and gave them nitrogen instead of air while Destiny tossed bottles into all the rooms. Then I went in after they passed out and put a drop in each one's eye. Their eyes were all pretty bloodshot but nowhere near monster red yet.

I hope Tammy's better soon, she's pretty busted up, damn them whores. We're lost without Tammy. The medic's readout said she'd had a very severe concussion, dislocated shoulder and a few broken ribs. At least she was awake now and the medic read "condition fair".

I should have let the robots clear the table, lunch was way past by now so when we were done we ate dinner... huh? Steak, baked potato, and salad. I hadn't hardly touched my salad at lunch. Huh? How the hell am I supposed to know what kind of damned potato, potatoes are potatoes as far as I'm concerned. The robots cooked them, anyway.

We had a bottle of wine to go along with it, but this time we only drank one bottle, then watched another *Rawhide* together, then a really, really dumb movie about California beaches from the nineteen sixties that we turned off after fifteen minutes and finished the *Star Wars* movie. I was surprised, this one wasn't as funny but it was still pretty good.

It was still early and the bottle was only half gone, so Destiny put on that old prison movie. Halfway through it she said yeah, that was from the book she was reading and "this one follows the book pretty close except it was Popeye fucking Olive Oyl in the book" and that they'd left a chapter or two out in the movie. She added "Except for the flies coming out of the big black prisoner's mouth, and the scene where the guy gets burned up, and the magic shit I thought it was good, even if it wasn't a hologram."

Then we put old music on and cuddled a long while and went to bed.

Chapter Forty Five

Captures

I got up about seven thirty or so, and Destiny was still asleep. I started coffee and told the robot to make breakfast, and then I shit, shaved, and got dressed in the clothes I'd worn the day before; I'd be nasty after engine inspections.

Destiny was still asleep and I had to be in the pilot room in fifteen minutes, so I started eating by myself. At five 'til I filled my coffee and took the rest of my breakfast to the pilot room. Huh? Eggs and bacon. What? Of course it was turkey bacon. Now knock it off before I walk out of here.

At a minute to eight I put it down, of course, and when readings were done I finished eating, and went back to my quarters to fill my coffee. If I told the stupid robots to get me a cup they'd pour the pot of good coffee down the drain and give me a cup of that nasty robot coffee. Stupid robots. Stupid robot *programmers*. What the hell is wrong with them? Ain't they never been on a boat? Don't they drink coffee?

I had another full inspection today since it had been too dangerous to inspect cargo the day before. I'd talked to Ramos, the fleet commander, about parts for the busted generator but he told me it would have to be fixed on Mars because nobody had the parts out here and it was going to have to be rebuilt in any case. At least the robots got the other one fixed with a part from another one of his boats. He said he could spare a few maids, which was a relief, it really stank downstairs. Maybe they'd have it cleaned up before we got to Mars.

Tammy came walking down the hallway, with her face still badly bruised and with her arm in a sling, looking like she was in pain. "The medic released you?" I asked.

"Yeah. It gave me a bottle of some kind of synthetic opiate but I'm not taking them, I need a clear mind. I'm taking Ibotrin."

"That better than naproxin?" I asked.

"Not much," she said. "Maybe a little. Look, I need to control the medics, I need readings on all the droppers and the computer says I don't have clearance for what I need to do. Can you fix that for me?"

"Yeah," I said, pulling out my fone. "Computer, give Doctor Winters complete access and command control to all medical robots for the, uh, duration of the trip."

"Acknowledged," It said.

"Thanks," she said.

"No," I said, "No need to thank me, you're trying to keep me and everybody else alive and you're researching how to cure monsters. Look, Tammy, I have to finish my inspec..." an alarm went off, it was Ramos. "Captain Knolls, it's Commander Ramos. There is pirate activity, what are your orders, sir?"

Sir? What the hell, I work for a living!

"Have you done this kind of thing before, Commander?"

"Yes, sir, we're very experienced. I studied at Annapolis and was a commander in the Marine Space Corps, and my men are all ex-military as well. And we've been seriously kicking some pirate ass lately, too, sir." There's that damned "sir" again.

"Good," I said, "your orders are to protect our people and property. Wait to transfer the robots until things quiet down."

"Yes sir."

"Don't call me sir, God damn it, I work for a living!"

"Yes si..., uh, yes, Captain Knolls.

"Call me John. What's your name?"

"Joe." I wondered what the whores would call him?

"Just do your job and we'll be okay, Joe. Okay?"

"Yes, Captain." Shit. Oh, well, these ate-up military guys never change. I know, I spent a hitch in the Army and all the lifers were ate up like that. I hear the Marines are the most ate up of all the military branches. Assholes...

I let Ramos worry about the pirates, that was his job now. I had a bunch of drug addicts that were all worse than vampires and werewolves to deal with. Lots more dangerous than stupid damned pirates, especially with a fleet and an experienced commander protecting us from the pirates and nobody but ourselves to protect us from the monsters. And I still had inspection. And I didn't know if Tammy had gotten them under control yet. Or even if she could all busted up like that.

Nope, not gonna inspect cargo today again, still way too damned dangerous, I don't care what the damned book says. I called Tammy and asked her to call me when the cargo pens were relatively safe.

Nothing caught fire when I inspected the empty passengers quarters that the company is stupid enough to power and have maids clean.

The starboard generator was fine, engine seventeen... damn it, the one that shorted out earlier and a robot was working on it. I unplugged it, sealed the plug hole with epoxy and told the computer to keep the damned robots away from it. I was done with everything before noon, except the damned cargo inspection. I wanted to hear from the doctor first.

Destiny was sitting on the couch watching the news with a cup of coffee when I got out of the shower. "You're a little early today," she remarked.

"I didn't inspect cargo," I said. "I want to make sure Tammy gets the monsters under control first. I'd inspect the Frankenstein monster's house before I'd inspect a dropless drophead's house. Damned addicts. Is there any good coffee left?"

"I just made another pot. Are you hungry?"

"I could eat. What are you having?"

"I don't know, maybe a grilled cheese sandwich and a bowl of potato soup."

I told the robot to make lunch and poured a cup of coffee and a glass of water.

We watched the news as we ate lunch. The news was talking about the Martian terraforming project. They had the hole halfway drilled and something went wrong and the machinery caught fire. It must have been built by the same morons that designed our old robots. Three people were in the hospital, one in critical condition.

The hole they were drilling was for a big magnet. The lady on the news said that without a magnetic field, a planet can't hold much of an atmosphere and there's no shield against solar and cosmic radiation.

The whole terraforming project was expected to take a few hundred more years to complete. Moving landfill from the asteroid belt and ice from Saturn's rings wasn't slated to start for another fifty years, but when it was done Mars would have Earth gravity or close, a similar atmosphere, lakes, rivers, and oceans, and they wouldn't need the domes any more.

Everyone on the Venus station was dead. They were debating what to do with it.

Commander Ramos called with news that the pirate boats had all been eradicated, fifteen had been captured and the crews put in detention. Damn, but he's good. Four of them were our company's boats, and eleven were from two other companies who would be paying us recovery fees. Hell, they did have some of our boats! I hadn't thought they could do that. Of course, they would have had mine if it wasn't for Tammy's monster blockade and then the fleet showing up.

Then Tammy called and said it was safe to inspect cargo pens, so I did. The German woman was in the commons eating and the rest were all sleeping, except Lek, who was apparently reading although I wouldn't be able to read it. It was obviously in Thai and they must have a completely different alphabet than us, because it was just squiggles to me.

I complimented her on her dress. She smiled weakly despite her bloodshot eyes; Tammy's book said she was in pretty much pain right now and no other drug would ease it. She would have to put a drop in soon, even though she didn't want to.

We would be docking at the repair facility the day after tomorrow, and the landing boats would already be docked there. Destiny and me would fly down in my houseboat.

It was finally safe to drink a beer or two. I went back to my quarters and opened one, and Destiny had the robot bring her one, too, and asked me what I wanted for dinner.

"I don't know, pork chops, caviar, and Champagne maybe?"

She laughed. "Yeah, on gold plates and silver cutlery! Fried chicken and mashed potatoes and broccoli sounds good to me, what are you having?"

"Chicken sounds good."

The robot fried the chicken and cooked the vegetables and wheeled over with the food. Robots make pretty damned good fried chicken, lots better than I can.

Then we watched some really weird movie from the end of the twenty first century, and went to bed. No, I don't know the name of the stupid movie.

Chapter Forty Six

Engines

We'd be in orbit around Mars and landing on the surface tomorrow. Only one more day of this horror movie! We might all live after all!

Destiny was still asleep. I got out of bed and went to the head, went in the kitchen to start coffee (stupid robots) and put a robe on.

Yeah, in that order. Fuck you.

Anyway, I told the robots to make me some breakfast. Destiny got up and went in the kitchen while I got dressed. The robot was almost done frying my eggs and sausage and had started cooking hers.

"Good morning!" she said. "Been up long?"

"'Mornin', sweetheart. Maybe ten minutes. Computer," I said, "What time is it?"

The table said "seven thirty three." I hate that table.

We ate our breakfast, then drank coffee and watched the news in the living room as the robots cleared the table. They were still trying to figure out what do do about Venus. It also had something about the battle the fleet fought, but Destiny said that they didn't mention me or her charity that the company was hauling for but they mentioned Bill's boat and its sabotage; I didn't get to see the whole thing. They had an interview with Mister Osbourne, but I had to go to the pilot room and I missed that part, too.

We didn't need a course correction, but there were red lights on engines sixteen and eighteen, right next to seventeen. I shut those two down and the two next to them as well and went to inspect them, stopping at home to fill my coffee. There was some politician talking about shipping and pirates on the news while I was there.

"Trouble?" Destiny asked, seeing my frown.

"Only a little, we have two more broken engines right next to seventeen. I'm going down to inspect them now."

I was astonished when I walked past the commons and saw Tammy talking to the German woman, and the German lady was actually wearing clothes!

I trudged down the five damned flights of stairs and inspected engines fifteen through nineteen first. Sixteen and eighteen had shorted out like seventeen, so I left fifteen and nineteen shut down as well in case it was something spreading from one engine to another like they seemed to have done on that Titan run, and I ordered the computer to leave all five alone. The book doesn't say to do that and I don't know how those engines work, but I saw a pattern here and I wasn't going to take any chances, anyway. I plugged repairbots in diagnostic mode into the four I'd shut off, hoping they wouldn't burn up and melt like the two that had tried to fix the dead number seventeen, but maybe they could record something engineering could use.

I logged it all, but the rest of the motors and the working generator were exactly like the tablet said they were supposed to be. Busy morning!

I trudged up all those damned stairs and took off my nasty boots and went straight to the shower. UGH! Damn but it was nasty down there.

I put on clean clothes and inspected cargo next. Yesterday's inspection was two days late, so I had to do it again, thankfully for the last time; no more inspections. Tomorrow morning we would dock at the repair facility and Destiny and me would leave on the houseboat, and the company's boat and the stench downstairs would be somebody else's problem. I couldn't wait to get off of that damned boat!

The only ones who were in their rooms were all asleep,

and the rest were in the commons, maybe thirty or so. It was noon, I was hungry, and decided to finish inspections after lunch.

"Done already?" Destiny asked.

"No, I was downstairs longer than normal. I still have to inspect the passenger section and the commons and the sick bay. Want to go for a walk with me after lunch? I'm starved."

"Sure," she said. "Robot, two rare ribeye steaks, mashed potatoes and gravy, and coleslaw."

We ate, and she came along as I finished my inspection. I did the commons last, and by then the only two people in there were Lek and the German woman. Lek was drinking coffee and the blonde was eating some kind of sandwich, and both of them were wearing clothes. I guess the blonde didn't want to be an animal, either. It was nice seeing people in the commons and nobody was naked for a change.

Destiny said "hello, ladies, I like your dresses." Lek said "Cup coon mock; oops, that Thai for 'thank you very much'."

The heavy German woman said "thank you" in her heavy German accent as well.

We were due to enter orbit around Mars the next morning, so Destiny came in the pilot room with me as I watched over the computers for our final approach. "You're going to be happy and the droppers are going to hate it," I said. "We'll be weightless when we enter orbit and dock tomorrow."

We had walked slowly and by then it was almost suppertime, so when I finished getting us ready to go into orbit we went home and had the robot make pizza and bring us each a beer. I'm getting used to Newcastle, I might keep drinking it on Mars. Well, I was going to have to drink Newcastle for a while anyway, because I still had an awful lot of it crammed in my houseboat. I don't get many chances to drink much of it on a journey. My boat's half full of beer!

After supper we moved our luggage to the houseboat, and Destiny put on the third *Lord of the Rings* movie and we ate the pizza while we watched the beginning of the movie, then we cuddled while we watched the rest of it.

Those are some a long movies! We listened to some Vaughn and then went to bed. I told the computer to wake me up at six.

Chapter Forty Seven

Landing

The alarm woke me up. Still asleep I thought "damned whores" out of habit, thinking we were having an emergency before I remembered that we were due to enter orbit and I'd set the alarm myself the night before. We had been on approach since late yesterday afternoon and would be in orbit and docking with the maintenance facility at nine this morning. The landing boats would already be docked there and we would be on Mars' surface by late this afternoon.

The alarm woke Destiny up, too, and she got up as I was making coffee. Destiny told the computer to make steak and scrambled eggs with toast, and we took a shower together.

Wow! We were finally entering orbit around Mars and would be docking at nine and we hadn't died! Not yet, at least. The way this trip had gone we'd probably crash land on Mars, or get assassinated at the spaceport. I did have a price on my head, after all. Of course, they most likely didn't know my name or what I looked like, but the boat's new captain would probably be in danger.

We put on the news and started eating breakfast and the doorbell rang. It was Tammy.

"Hi, Tammy," Destiny said. "Want some breakfast?"

"No, thanks," she said, "I already ate, but I'll take a cup of coffee if it isn't made by a robot. So, who's going to be your bridesmaid?"

"Well, who do you think, silly," Destiny said. "You, of course. Who's going to be your best man, John?"

"Bill, of course, but he won't be here for a week or

more, he's on batteries."

They started talking about clothes and I just kind of zoned out and nodded once in a while.

At five 'til eight I went in the pilot room to finish getting us in orbit, and by eight thirty we were weightless and would be docking in a few minutes. I floated to my quarters.

At quarter to nine the three of us started floating towards the docking bay that still worked without tearing up somebody else's docking bay and didn't have my boat attached, so we could meet the landing crafts' captains who would escort passenger and cargo to Mars. Then we'd take off in the houseboat and Tammy would go down with the droppers.

I got on the PA. "Attention, ladies. Please assemble in docking bay one for landing."

The boat docked a few minutes later as the droppers started showing up, and I greeted two of the three landing pilots, Tom Farley and Jim Woolsley. I'd known both of them for a few years, so we talked about old times as Destiny and Tammy said their goodbyes and cargo streamed in.

They and Tammy started escorting the droppers to the landing boats while me and Destiny went to my houseboat to land on Mars. Lek walked by and said "Thank you, Captain."

We undocked from the ship and flew down to Meridian Bay Spaceport together. Now if you guys will excuse me I need to buy a wedding ring.

See you.

Chapter Forty Eight

Mars!

Dewey was on his way to Mars when he finished reading Knolls' report. He sipped on the coffee the captain had brought and switched on the news. They were digging the deep hole in Mars again.

Plans were being made to tow the tragic Venus station to drop into the sun. It had been argued that if they dropped it on Venus it would incinerate from the friction with Venus' thick carbon dioxide atmosphere, but some lesser educated people were afraid that the disease might somehow survive Venus' hellish surface.

Charles was back on the video talking about pirates. He was glad it was Charles and not him, Dewey hated video cameras.

He emailed Kowalski, telling him that when Kelly got back to Earth to have a couple of his best electrical engineers, one who was good with batteries and one that was good with engines, to talk to him and find out how he got a third gravity out of batteries. Nobody else had managed to do that before, and some engineers claimed it was physically impossible.

John and Destiny had left the houseboat parked on a space port pad they had rented at the spaceport at the Meridian Bay dome and got in a cab. Destiny had said "I don't want to shop on an empty stomach. Taxi, take us to a restaurant that serves eggs and pork sausage this time of day."

"Wow," John said. "That's going to be an expensive place."

"Well, I'm buying. You said you never tried pork

sausage, now's your chance, it's my treat. Besides, I've been thinking about pork sausage for half the trip and I don't want to wait any longer!"

They were really busy on Mars the next few days, mostly shopping. First shopping for a wedding ring, then for real estate; they would buy a house and a bar. The houseboat was big as houseboats go, but was a bit small for someone as wealthy as Destiny who had lived all her life in very large homes, especially since the houseboat was half full of beer.

After signing papers for the house they went for breakfast at a nice restaurant, where Destiny bought John another omelette and pork sausage. John wasn't any more impressed with this sausage than at the other restaurant.

Then they visited Tammy in her hotel room. Her face was still a little bruised but she wasn't wearing the sling.

"Hi, come on in, guys. Want some coffee?"

"Sure," Destiny said. "So how are you coming with your research?"

"Well, we haven't had time to do much except move them into the facility and acquaint them with it, but Rilla had really come a long way and Lek was almost cured already, at least from the physical withdrawal symptoms, by the time we got to Mars. She's to the point that withdrawal is still torture to her, but no longer deadly. She's still in mental and physical pain but she's not dropping any more. The physical pain should be gone in a few weeks. Of course, full therapy will probably take years."

John said "Yes, Lek sure did change during the trip. This is great coffee, Tammy!"

She laughed. "It's robot coffee!"

"No way," John said.

"Yep, and it's one of your company's robots that made it, too!"

"No way in hell!" John exclaimed.

"It's true," she said. "Your company updated all their coffeebots' operating systems and other programs. And it perks a whole pot of coffee in five minutes, and a cup in less than a minute. You have one of their robots, now it can make good coffee. I only found out because they're advertising it all over everywhere. I'm surprised you didn't notice."

"I saw the ads, I just didn't believe them."

Destiny laughed. "Dad must have tried a cup of his own robots' nasty coffee, I think he fired his head engineer. He should get here in another week."

John said "Bill lands in two days. I'm still reeling from the trip here. God, but that was a damned nightmare!"

They continued chatting a while before going home to the houseboat, still parked at the spaceport. They would be moving into their new home about the time Bill showed up two days later and would have more shopping to do; they would need furniture, curtains, and so forth.

John and Destiny met him at the spaceport, and they stopped at a bar for the beer he'd promised John. He bought John and Destiny several, in fact.

"Excuse me, Bartender, but I want to buy a round," John said. The bartender told John what they cost.

"Wow," he said. "That's pretty high! Is it like that everywhere here?"

The bartender told him the reason was the cost of shipping it to Mars from Earth. He was going to clean up in the tavern business, it seemed, since Destiny would get a huge discount on shipping. He decided that while he was learning business he'd learn how to make beer and open a microbrewery in his tavern, too. He'd have really cheap beer, at least compared to other taverns, that he could sell for a huge profit and still be way cheaper than anyone else's if he could learn to make good beer.

Bill said "Bartender, don't take his money, this is all on me.

"I have to write a damned report tomorrow, I don't know why," he said, turning to John.

"I had to write one and they really wanted detail," John

said. "Maybe they changed policies and everybody has to write reports now."

A few days after that they met Dewey at the spaceport. After Dewey and his daughter hugged she said "Where's Mom?"

Dewey said "Come on, Destiny, you know how your mom is. She's scared to death to even get on an airplane, let alone a space ship. I'm going to wear a camera at the wedding, though, so she'll be there in a way."

He stuck out his hand. "Good seeing you again, John. That was some great work you did on that trip. Between you and Commander Ramos and his fleet there are only a quarter as many pirates left. We're going to be rewriting the book. I wish I could talk you out of retiring."

"Well, thank you, Mister Green..."

"Call me Dewey, John. You're family now."

Notes

Chapter one: In the summer of 2013 I was in the beer garden at Felber's Tavern, a little redneck bar in the ghetto, talking with Dewey Green and a couple of other guys about *Nobots*, which he'd just read. A half dozen crack whores walked down the street, and Dewey commented "you ought to write a book about whores in space."

I didn't recall ever reading a science fiction story about whores in space before. It took a couple of months to figure out a plot where whores in space would make sense, and it seemed a challenge to write.

Dewey wanted me to name a character after him, so the CEO is named Dewey Green. Charles Osbourne is named after Dewey's dad Charles and his grandfather Osbourne.

Chapter two: Since I have no editors or proofreaders, editing is the hardest part of writing. I have to fret over stuff like "is it who or whom", or other grammatical blunders. I thought that since most of this was going to be from the first person perspective of someone who would be a roofer or a bricklayer today, I thought it would be a piece of cake.

I was wrong, I discovered that bad grammar and a limited vocabulary are hard to do! Sometimes I'd sit at the keyboard for half an hour trying in vain to find a short synonym for a multisyllable word that Knolls would never use.

Chapter five: If it had been a first class flight, Knolls would have ridden his houseboat to the ship while the rich passengers rode a space plane.

Chapter eight: Before 1949, cataracts usually meant blindness, although there were surgical techniques to alleviate the condition. In 1949 the Intraocular lens was developed in England, which cured not only the cataract, but nearsightedness and astigmatism as well. However, the patient still needed reading glasses.

In 2003 a new type of IOL was developed that can restore better than 20/20 vision at all distances in many patients. I had one inserted in 2006, and at age 62 need no corrective lenses at all after a lifetime of being extremely nearsighted, as well as being farsighted after middle age.

In the next few hundred years techniques and equipment will surely advance greatly. Most likely, folks with IOLs will probably have better vision than Destiny had after her surgery.

Chapter nine: In the US in the nineteen twenties, only the very rich could afford chicken. Anyone who had chickens needed them for the eggs, and would only sell them for a very high price.

In the campaign for the 1928 US Presidential election, Herbert Hoover's campain slogan was "A chicken in every pot and a car in every garage", meaning that everyone would be prosperous during his presidency.

The stock market crashed on October 24, 1929, plunging the country into what is called "The Great Depression".

Chapter Thirteen: I researched drug-addicted prostitutes by haunting the sleaziest bars in town (one has been closed by the health department) and talking to them. The addicts in the book are based on what I learned in sleazy bars.

Chapter fifteen: What Knolls, who doesn't know how the thrusters work, doesn't understand is that they don't just run on electricity, they expel ions at a high velocity. The ionized material is the actual fuel, and takes up most of the five story tall motors. He guesses correctly that it does indeed have something to do with maintenance, since the fuel is part of the motor and is built in.

Chapter seventeen: The maid must have broken down hours earlier than it had caught fire, since they clean at noon.

It is mentioned that the clocks reset when they get to Mars; this is because of the time dilation caused by the extreme speeds you would reach at .3 to .7 gravities thrust. Space captains and frequent travelers would live a very long time, since the faster you go, the slower time goes (depending on the perspective of the observer, whether the traveler or someone stationary).

Chapter eighteen: An EMP is an electromagnetic pulse, which will break anything that's transistorized.

Chapter nineteen: The title is in Thai, and translates to "catfight".

I spent a year in Thailand while stationed there in the USAF. They were the friendliest people I ever met. I became friends with quite a few, where I heard that prostitutes are honored in Thailand, although I don't know if that's actually true.

When Thai women argue, they do indeed sound like cats fighting. Interestingly, they have a legend that once people were happy and lived in harmony, but then the evil felines taught us to talk and we've been arguing and fighting ever since.

"Meow" really is Thai for "I want." "Money" is just as coincidentally Thai for "come here."

John mentions that he can't tell the difference between the two Leks' names, and that went both ways. The Thai words for "you" and "me" both sound like "coon" to me. A black friend once tried to teach me the difference and we wound up laughing so hard we gave up. There are sounds in their language that we simply don't have, like starting a word with "ng". There are sounds in our language theirs doesn't have as well, such as the "st" combination or the letter V. I only met one Thai who could pronounce my first name, Steve. It came out as "Teeb".

The town John thought was "Bong Chong" was named (and of course this is phonetic) *Bahnchang.* It sat between the Thai naval base (that we Americans were renting part of to launch B-52s from to bomb Vietnam) in the country's south, and another town named *Sadaheep.* I rented a bungalow in Bahnchang.

Chapter twenty: John didn't have to worry about losing the computers. As an astrophysicist, Destiny knew calculus and could have done the calculations necessary for getting them to Mars.

Chapter twenty five: When John had the expensive BLT, the restaurant obviously swindled him, since turkey bacon doesn't, in fact, taste like pork bacon.

Language will change far more in the next few hundred years than the spelling of "phone". John wonders why people "hang up" their "fones", but it's doubtless that the only things getting hung up by then are clothing.

www.ingramcontent.com/pod-product-compliance
Lightning Source LLC
Chambersburg PA
CBHW030411020726
47493CB00003B/1030